Murder at Mistletoe Manor

The Wootton Windmill Mysteries
Book 7

Izzie Harper

ASIN for the ebook: B0D9FHLZ6H

ISBN for the paperback: 978-1-7392189-6-6

For Lesley Cowan, RIP.

Chapter 1 Day 1 THURSDAY

Snow had been falling all day in the village of Lower Wootton. The pavements and roads were covered with a glistening, white blanket. Sylvia and Ellie Blix were wandering round the Christmas market with other families, buying gifts and waiting for the official switching-on of the lights at 5pm. Carols played over a sound system. The roofs of the German-style, wooden huts were laden with snow, and a range of delicious aromas wafted on the wind: fruity mulled wine; sweet hot chocolate; spicy sausages and fried onions.

'Fancy a Glühwein?' asked Sylvia, dragging out the 'oo' to mimic a German accent. She tightened her scarf against the cold wind and tucked it into her coat.

'Mmm,' replied Ellie. 'But I haven't eaten since lunchtime. Think I'll grab a sausage first.'

To their left, a child squealed in delight as her mother passed her a bag of candy floss.

Sylvia and Ellie approached the sausage stall and Ellie started reading the descriptions on the menu. 'Bratwurst... made of veal, beef and pork.' She slid her bobble hat off, let out her ponytail and arranged her hair loosely round her neck. Then pulled her hat back on.

'I've had that before,' Sylvia replied. 'Tasty.'

'Weisswurst, made of minced veal and back bacon,' Ellie continued. 'That sounds nice. Leberwurst: liver, thyme, mustard seeds and nutmeg.'

Sylvia nudged her. 'You've got me wanting one now.'

'Knackwurst is beef and garlic,' Ellie continued. 'Bockwurst is the Frankfurter we can get in the shops here.'

'Shall we get a different one each and share? That way we get to taste two.'

They made their decision and paid, and were soon shuffling along the high street, stuffing sausage into their mouths and chatting.

It was a week before Christmas and one of Sylvia's favourite times of year. As they approached the pretzel stall, the library came into view. It was a single storey building with a flat roof, set back from the high street with a small square in front. Outside, coloured fairy lights flickered on a Christmas tree, sending shards of red, green and blue onto the surrounding people and building.

Sylvia checked her watch for the second time. Where was Penelope Wyndham? It wasn't like her to be late. Sylvia remembered the time Penelope had come to the bakery book club to give a talk about her children's fiction. Eighteen months ago, or thereabouts, before she moved back to the village. Penelope had arrived half an hour early, while the hosts were putting out chairs and setting up refreshments. She'd expected everyone to stop what they were doing and get her a seat and a drink.

Sylvia chuckled to herself. Her late husband had always said that some people swooped on celebrity while others kept it at a distance. She took the last mouthful of her mulled wine. Whoever had made it used more cinnamon and clove than she did. She'd experiment with another batch tomorrow.

O come all ye faithful was playing through speakers and Sylvia found herself singing along to the chorus.

'O come, let us adore him.'

It shouldn't really matter that Penelope was late. They were all going to her home, Mistletoe Manor, afterwards for drinks and canapés, so they could simply start whenever they arrived. If the children in the village were late to bed, it didn't matter too much. They didn't have school tomorrow.

'O come, let us adore him...'

And it wasn't as if Sylvia could do anything about Penelope's arrival. The older woman didn't have a mobile phone so ringing her wasn't an option. They would just have to wait. She would be here in a minute. The only issue was that it was chilly, standing about, waiting, particularly for the older members of the village.

She glanced around. Children scampered about excitedly. They wouldn't get cold.

'Have I got time to nip and get us another cup of mulled wine, do you think?' Sylvia asked Ellie. 'It's mainly fruit juice, isn't it? Practically one of our five-a-day.' She chuckled mischievously.

'Go on then,' Ellie replied, checking her phone. 'I'm wondering about my bed and breakfast guests. They got caught in traffic and haven't arrived yet.'

But home was only a few minutes' walk up the road. Ellie could get back to the windmill at any stage and check them in.

On her way, Sylvia chatted to neighbours about their plans for Christmas, their families, the stalls, the snow and the imminent lights.

Then cries of excitement went up. 'She's here.' The crowd cheered loudly and clapped.

A horn tooted. Wheels crunched on the snow and a silver, stretch limousine came into view and pulled up.

'Here she is.'

Two people on stilts approached the vehicle. One was Sylvia's granddaughter, Zoe. The other was Zoe's boyfriend.

'Those things scare the living daylights out of me,' Sylvia told Ellie as she rejoined her, her face scrunched in worry. 'Particularly in the snow.' She handed Ellie a steaming paper cup and pointed at the elongated legs of the stilt walkers. 'I know they've been having lessons, but still...'

Fruit and spice wafted up Sylvia's nose as she took a sip of the warm wine.

Over by the limo, the driver's door opened. The chauffeur got out, a man in a black suit and a peaked cap. He opened a back door, and a woman stepped out, wearing a low-cut, black dress with a fur jacket over her shoulders. Letter-box red lipstick. Legs in black tights and stiletto shoes.

'Very Penelope,' whispered Sylvia. 'Hope she's safe in those shoes. I'd be on my bottom in seconds.'

Penelope gave an understated, sideways wave.

'She's got that regal look down, hasn't she?' said Ellie. 'Looks more like an A-list film star than a retired author.'

'The press didn't call her "Lady Penelope" for nothing,' Sylvia told her. 'My Ron said his whole CID team even started using that name for her when they were investigating her husband.'

Zoe and Finn escorted Penelope to the 'switch' that had been rigged up on a table by the village electrician, outside the library in the square.

A new carol had started. *'Jingle bells, jingle bells, jingle all the way,'* it tinkled.

Penelope got settled in front of the table and reached for the switch, pausing and looking up at the audience.

Another cheer went up and she beamed.

Dave smiled at his mum and Ellie from across the street, and waved. At least *he* wasn't going to be cold in his Santa outfit and beard. He and Ellie had arranged a pizza date for that evening, and Sylvia knew Ellie was looking forward to it.

Zoe leaned over, touched Penelope's shoulder and asked, 'Ready?'

Penelope nodded.

The crowd took their cue and began chanting.

'Ten, nine, eight...'

Overhead, a crescent moon watched over them.

'... six, five...'

Stars glimmered in the blue sky.

'... three... two...'

Cloud wisps floated.

'... ONE.'

Cheers went up as Penelope flicked the switch and the high street was drenched in soft white light. In an arch, high above the street, fairy lights shone brightly, some flickering at intervals. Others ran along the outside of the gutters of the shops.

Sylvia watched as Penelope glanced around, smiling and surveying the faces of all the people from the village who stood in front of her. She truly was Lady of the Manor. She said something to Zoe, who frowned briefly and leaned over, probably trying to hear her better over the cheers and the carols.

People quickly began chatting again and mingling, pointing at the lights, agreeing how pretty they looked, how striking the angels were at the top of the arches.

'Is she planning on staying, or what?' Ellie voiced the question that had popped into Sylvia's mind.

'Doubt it,' Sylvia replied. 'We've got the party in an hour. I imagine she'll want to get back to the manor house.'

Penelope raised her arm in the air and clicked her fingers at her chauffeur.

'There we go,' said Sylvia. 'Doesn't look like she's keen on mixing with the peasants.'

Ellie sniggered.

'I said I'd get a lift back with her,' Sylvia continued. 'Help get the food that needs heating into the oven in time for when everyone arrives.' Sylvia had done the catering for Penelope. 'But I rather fancy walking. I'll go over and tell her.'

Ellie's phone pinged and she skimmed the message. 'I'd better go. My guests have just arrived and aren't sure whether to nip into the Windmill Inn for a swift half or wait for me.' She stuffed her phone in her pocket. 'I'll get them settled and join you over at Mistletoe Manor. Hopefully there will still be some fizz and some of your prawn and cream cheese canapés left by then.'

'I'll keep you some. Don't worry. See you there.' Sylvia stomped through the snow to Penelope, who was still waving and smiling benevolently while locals snapped photos of the village celebrity.

'That went well,' Sylvia told her, shouting over the noise.

The two women made polite conversation for a few moments.

'Shall we head off now?' asked Penelope. 'I've had enough of crowds.'

Sylvia resisted the temptation to tut. 'It's such a lovely evening, I'm going to walk. I'll see you there.'

They said goodbye and Sylvia weaved through the crowd, along the high street. She was soon on her own, away from the bustle and noise. Snowflakes fluttered across her face, briefly cold and wet on her skin. The forecast was for continued snow and cold temperatures, and a white Christmas was on the cards. The fresh fall lay thick on the ground. Sylvia was grateful for the warm socks and walking boots that she and Ellie had put on.

Sylvia turned into the entrance of Mistletoe Manor's grounds and started walking up the sweeping drive. The large, wrought iron gates were open, ready for the guests.

It was an imposing building, dating back to the seventeenth century, built from Kent ragstone. Mistletoe Manor was the nickname it had acquired due to the lime and ash trees at the front of the house, whose canopies were host to the plant in winter. Its real name was Wootton Manor.

From her recent visits, helping with the catering, Sylvia knew the building was set on a sprawling estate with a pond, stables and tennis courts. For hundreds of years the place had been owned by the aristocratic Selby family, lords of the manor. As far as she knew, they still owned it, and Penelope was renting it for six months.

As Sylvia strode up the drive, she debated whether to ring at the front door or go round the back, as Penelope often liked her to do. The stretch limo was back in place outside the entrance, so Penelope was obviously home.

Sylvia decided on the main entrance, so she walked up the steps, admiring the stone pillars and giant doors. She pressed the buzzer and a deep, clanging bell sounded inside. But no-one came. She waited a few moments and tried again. Still no-one came.

Perhaps Penelope had nipped to the loo? Never mind, the chauffeur-come-housekeeper, Hargrave, was always around. She tried the bell a third time and decided to go round the back. The kitchen door was often open.

Once there, she knocked, this time with her hand on one of the back door's glass panels. 'Hello,' she called out. 'It's Sylvia.'

Maybe Hargrave was bringing in logs and making the fire in the Great Hall? She'd let herself in and get on with the preparations. Switch the ovens on.

She pushed down the handle of the panelled door and entered the kitchen. But instead of warm air and delicious cooking smells greeting her, there was a waft of cold.

'Penelope? Are you there? I'll put the food in to heat.'

Silence. And not just that. There was a sense of stillness in the house; a feeling that no one was here. Hargrave and Penelope couldn't have both gone out, surely?

Sylvia strode into the hall, continuing to call Penelope's name. It was possible the older woman hadn't heard her, of course. The thick, stone walls of the old building would conceal most noises. She would go and find Penelope. The first place to look was her bedroom.

Sylvia kicked off her walking boots and pushed them to the edge of the banisters, every sound echoing in the vast space. Then she made her way up the winding staircase, with its deep steps and thick carpet, past the family portraits on the walls.

Penelope's room was the second on the right, at the top of the stairs.

'Penelope? Are you up here?' Sylvia knocked loudly on the door. But no answer came so she pushed it open. The room was empty. A long, white, evening gown was hanging on the back of a wardrobe. On the floor underneath it was a pair of sparkly, white stilettos and a fascinator.

Sylvia crossed the bedroom, heading for the en-suite bathroom. But this was empty too. No tub full of steaming water and bubble bath. No towels, robes or clothes ready for use. In fact, there were no signs of life at all.

Before she went back downstairs, she called out again and knocked on the other doors on the upstairs landing. None of the four rooms which were open showed signs of occupation. One room was locked.

She made her way into the Great Hall where the reception was going to be. It was a huge space, originally used by the lord of the manor for receiving guests, dining and hosting parties.

The door was heavy and stiff, and creaked as Sylvia pushed it open. Her gaze fell on the long table, laid out for drinks with bottles of red wine and glasses. Champagne flutes. Silver buckets awaiting ice for white wine and fizz. Stacks of paper plates, Christmas crackers and party poppers. Nearby, several dozen books sat in piles on a table, all brightly-coloured hardbacks – and identical.

But as Sylvia's gaze shifted, she saw... something was wrong.

The Christmas tree was on its side on the floor, the lights half-off. A mahogany sideboard had been cleared of everything that was on it: white tablecloth; crystal glasses and decanters; vases of flowers. All lay higgledy-piggledy on the parquet. Everything from the mantelpiece was on the floor by the hearth: the clock, a candelabra lamp, pinecones and baubles.

What on earth had happened? Where was Penelope?

Sylvia approached the chaise longue, which was also on its side. And then she saw Penelope, lying on her back in the same dress she'd been wearing in the village, eyes bulging, a string of fairy lights pulled tight around her neck.

Chapter 2

Sylvia grabbed her phone, swiped the screen and dialled 999. She wasn't certain whether Penelope was dead or not, but it certainly looked like it, and there was no way she could have strangled herself; so this was now a crime scene, and she shouldn't touch anything – let alone Penelope. The paramedics would soon be here. They could check for signs of life.

As she waited for the emergency services operator to answer, Sylvia stepped away from the body, trying to think clearly in spite of the hammering in her chest. Passing the fallen sideboard, a notepad caught her attention on the floor. A few feet away from it, a biro lay amongst an array of items, some broken, some intact. The notepad had writing on it.

Turkey crown.

Stuffing.

Sausages.

Fizz.

Christmas pudding.

Then a large capital '*L*'.

What did that mean?

Sylvia gave all her information to the 999 operator and warned them guests were due to arrive any minute.

Before she left, she took a quick snap of the note with her phone, just in case Ellie or Zoe asked her what exactly it said. What might Penelope have been about to write? Lemons? Loo roll? Lightbulbs? If it was just her shopping list, there probably wasn't any point thinking too much about it.

She made her way to the front door to wait for the first responders to arrive. The police would contact Penelope's husband and family. What an awful shock it was going to be for them all.

She tried to think back to her conversations with Penelope when they'd discussed the food for the reception. Sylvia knew she had a husband, but had Penelope mentioned any other family? Not that Sylvia could remember. And she hadn't said much about her husband, either. Her comments had been vague when Sylvia asked if he'd be joining her for Christmas. Perhaps that was deliberate. After all, Sylvia's late husband had been responsible for his conviction.

Her thoughts were running away from her. It wasn't going to help.

But try as she might, two questions kept popping into her mind: was the letter on the notepad relevant or just a note that Penelope had been making for herself? And where was Hargrave, the chauffeur?

Chapter 3

'Here you go, Gran,' said Zoe, passing Sylvia a mug of steaming hot chocolate.

Ellie typed a quick text to Dave saying she would have to cancel their pizza date. Shame. She had been looking forward to it. He'd probably got roped into the investigation though and wouldn't be able to make it himself.

Sylvia was on the couch in the living room at the windmill with Ellie and Zoe. She had two cushions behind her back, a furry throw over her legs and Tallulah-the-tabby on her lap. She took a gulp of the warm, sweet liquid. 'Crikey.' She smacked her lips together and grinned. 'What did you put in that? Rum?'

'Medicine, Gran.' Zoe winked mischievously. 'Isn't that what *you* call it?'

'I can't believe poor Penelope had fairy lights round her neck,' said Ellie, who was sitting cross-legged on the floor. Rebus was beside her, playing with the other kitten, Cleopatra.

'That's got to be murder,' said Zoe.

Sylvia nodded.

'You're sure there was no one else in the house?' asked Zoe.

Sylvia shook her head, explaining how many times she'd called out. That she'd checked all the rooms but one. 'Unless they were in there... or hiding.'

'That does seem strange, doesn't it?' said Zoe. 'Particularly since the limo was outside and guests were shortly going to be arriving for the reception. What did Dad say?'

Dave was a detective inspector in the local police.

'He asked me to go through what happened when I arrived at the house; what I noticed and heard and saw. I told him about the notepad, but by then the crime scene staff had already arrived and were recording and preserving all the evidence. Several people were asking him for instructions, so he said he'll pop round when he has a moment to ask me some more questions.'

'What an awful thing to happen,' said Ellie. 'And at Christmas too.'

'I feel bad,' said Sylvia, her voice breaking as she spoke. 'I didn't particularly like Penelope, but I was the person who found her. Plus – I was one of the last people to see her alive.'

Rebus must've caught the emotion in Sylvia's tone, as he jumped onto the sofa and squidged between her and the back of the cushions.

She gave him an appreciative stroke, then screwed up her nose. 'Have you been rolling in fox poo?' She moved him around to check his fur.

'It's me, I'm afraid,' said Zoe apologetically. 'We had to pick up a poorly fox earlier.' She gestured to her trousers.

'Ew.' Sylvia held her nose dramatically. 'Get them off and into the washing machine.'

'I will in a minute. You were telling us about Penelope...'

'Yes. If I'd got there earlier, whoever killed her might not have been able to get access to her. Or if I'd gone back to the manor house in the limo, it also might not have happened. If only I hadn't insisted on walking.' She let out a regretful sigh.

'You can't think like that,' Ellie told her. 'I know what you mean, but it's not your fault she's dead. The only person responsible is the one who killed her.'

It was just after 8pm. Apart from the sausages at the market, none of them had eaten. Were they hungry? She wasn't. She was about to ask how the others felt when a woman's voice interrupted her musings.

'Er... hi-i.'

They looked round and saw Ellie's B&B guest, a tall, glamorous woman in a onesie and sheepskin slippers.

'Sorry to interrupt but is it possible to get some extra sugar? My husband has three in his tea, and we've gone through the current supply already.' She rolled her eyes affectionately. 'I've offered him my sweeteners, but he won't touch the stuff.'

'Of course.' Ellie got to her feet. 'How are you settling in? Is the room OK for you?' She ambled across the lounge and into the kitchen.

Zoe looked up, presumably curious to know what the woman was going to say about her bedroom.

'Yes, lovely, thank you. We're from London so snowy fields and villages are a novelty for us. Stunning views. You can see lights from the ships on the sea.'

Ellie passed the woman a handful of sugar sachets. 'You alright for milk and cookies too? We've got plenty.'

'Yes, thanks. What a beautiful home you have here. Have you been doing bed and breakfast lo–?' She broke off, her nose curling as she sniffed the air.

Zoe must've caught the gesture. 'Sorry. Is it the smell? It's my trousers. I'll take them off now.' She headed for the office, where they kept the clean laundry.

The guest stared after Zoe, clearly taken aback.

'Around three months. My daughter...' Ellie gestured towards the office, 'moved in with her boyfriend and his friend. They've got a big house in the village. And I've been thinking about hosting B&B guests for a number of years.'

Zoe reappeared in a pair of Ellie's jogging bottoms. She took her smelly work trousers over to the washing machine and rejoined them in the lounge.

'Oh, I see. We thought you must've done it for ages. All the little touches in the room: the chocolates, flowers. My hubby is a fan of the Teasmade.'

Ellie smiled, pleased her efforts were appreciated. 'At one time, my husband and I were contemplating converting the outhouse in the garden into accommodation.'

'If you don't mind me asking, is your daughter the first to flee the nest?' She pointed at Zoe. 'My son went to university a couple of months ago. I miss him like crazy.'

'We haven't had much time to miss this one,' said Sylvia wryly, from her place on the couch. 'She might not sleep here, but she spends as much time here as she always did. As does her boyfriend.'

The B&B guest chuckled.

'Gran. That's not very nice. You and Mum said I could come back whenever I wanted.'

Ellie caught the hurt in her daughter's voice.

'And you've always loved Finn,' Zoe continued.

'You *can*, lovey,' said Ellie. 'Your gran's just joking. Don't take any notice. She's had a nasty shock.' She turned back to the guest. 'Anyway, you won't hear me complaining. I get to have B&B guests, make some extra money *and* see my daughter regularly.'

'I'm Bridget, by the way,' the woman said. 'Incidentally – do you know what's going on out there? We saw a load of police cars earlier. Flashing lights, sirens, an ambulance. They seemed to be heading towards that big manor house at the end of the village. One of the barmaids in the pub next door told us that a retired children's author lives there. Is that right?'

'Live-*d*', Sylvia shouted over again from the lounge, emphasising the 'd' of the past tense. 'Penelope Wyndham. Sadly, she's just been–'

'What part of London are you from?' Ellie changed the subject quickly, worried her guests might be alarmed by Sylvia's excess of information.

'Bloomsbury. We're real townies.' Alarm returned to Bridget's elegant features. 'You said "lived". I hope nothing's happened to her. Nigel – that's my husband – says he thought there'd been a murder. The barmaid said people were turning up at the house, expecting a party. The police had to close the gates.'

'Oh dear,' Ellie replied noncommittally, returning to the lounge so she could hear Sylvia and Zoe without shouting. She wasn't sure what to tell Bridget, who was following her, so as not to worry her further.

'Your husband's correct, unfortunately,' said Sylvia. 'She's been killed.'

'Oh, my goodness. That's terrible.' Bridget's voice had started to squeak. 'What happened?'

'We don't know yet,' Sylvia replied. 'The police were there when I left.'

'You were *there*?' Her eyebrows shot up. 'Did you see it?'

Ellie gave Sylvia what she hoped was a silencing look. 'No. The police will find out what happened. We can leave it to them.'

Zoe piped up. 'Can we talk about Penelope Wyndham for a minute? I want to know how you ended up agreeing to do her catering, Gran, when Grandad put her husband behind bars?'

'Wait. What?' asked Bridget, who seemed to be part-fascinated and part-freaked out. '*Who* put *who* behind bars?'

Zoe explained, then carried on talking to Sylvia. 'You fudged the issue last time we asked you.'

Bridget stood, eyes wide, clearly alarmed by the events that were unfolding in the sleepy village they'd chosen for their stay.

Sylvia sighed. 'It's quite simple. I bumped into Penelope in the bakery. Kathy had asked me to make some of my frangipane mince pies for the shop. And Penelope came in to order a Christmas cake. She and Kathy got chatting about the switching-on of the Christmas lights, and she asked Kathy if she knew anyone who could help her with making a few canapés for the reception she was hosting afterwards. Kathy suggested me and, before I knew it, Penelope was talking as though everything was agreed.'

'You could have said no, though,' Zoe added.

'I know. I feel a bit bad now, given what's happened, but to be honest I let her bamboozle me because I was flattered and a bit... well... curious.'

'What about?' Ellie and Zoe chorused.

'What she was up to; why she'd come back to the village when it's where her husband was arrested. What was going on with her husband, and also whether I could make professional standard canapés after all this ti–'

A rap at the door brought their conversation to an abrupt halt.

Rebus barked and shot off the sofa.

'It's probably the cops, to take a statement from you, Gran. Or Dad.'

But it wasn't...

Ellie grabbed Rebus' collar and opened the door to a short woman who was enveloped by a long, khaki Parka. A woolly hat obscured her hair.

She fixed an angry gaze on Ellie. 'Are you Mrs Blix?'

'One of them, yes. How can I help?' Ellie had sensed it wasn't a friendly visit.

'*Sylvia* Blix?'

'No. That's my mother-in-law. Sorry, I don't think we've met. You are...?'

'Rebecca Wyndham. Penelope's daughter. The police said Sylvia found my mother. Could I speak to her?'

Ellie wasn't sure what to do. She had B&B guests in earshot of the conversation, Sylvia was on the sofa, in shock, and Rebecca's mother had just been killed.

Ellie smiled kindly. Whatever this woman was here for, she'd just lost her mother. 'We're all terribly sorry for your loss. We saw Penelope earlier, at the switching-on of the lights.'

'Thank you. But it's Sylvia I'd like to speak to, please.'

'It's OK,' Sylvia shouted from the lounge. 'I'm happy to talk to her.'

Ellie stood back and allowed the young woman to come in.

She pulled her woolly hat off and a curtain of mousey hair swept down on to her shoulders. She kicked off trendy, mustard-coloured walking boots and followed

Ellie over to the sofa. She seemed familiar but Ellie couldn't place where from.

'Was my dad at the house when you got there?'

'Not that I saw, no. There didn't seem to be anyone there apart from your mother.'

'What about that chauffeur chap? Was he not there either?'

Sylvia explained to Rebecca. She'd called out several times when she arrived; then upstairs. No one answered.

'Was she expecting your father for Christmas?' asked Ellie, trying to figure out what had been going on at the manor house.

Rebecca shot an irritated glance in Ellie's direction. 'I've got no idea what she arranged with him. Their relationship was very odd.'

Ellie and Sylvia caught each other's eye. That was a telling reply.

'Aren't you in touch with him, then?' asked Sylvia.

Rebecca ignored her question. 'There's something else though. I heard you guys run some sort of private detective agency.'

Ellie braced, hoping Rebecca wasn't going to ask them to investigate Penelope's death.

'Think you're the Miss Marples of the village...'

Rebus growled.

'I don't want to be rude or anything, but my family's been through enough. I absolutely do *not* want you poking around in my mother's death. Is that clear?'

Chapter 4 Day 2 FRIDAY

The next morning, Ellie was up by 6.30am. After Penelope's death, and the visit from Rebecca, she hadn't slept well, but the day beckoned and she had a list of jobs as long as her arm.

First of all, while Rebus was in the garden, she fed the kittens, made a cup of tea and checked the Blix Blitz diary. All the cleaning jobs were allocated and none of her staff had called in sick. Then she laid out breakfast items for her B&B guests, along with a note saying she'd be back by eight o'clock to cook their 'full English'. She didn't start her day with a fry-up, so it was something she'd had to get used to: buying good quality bacon and sausages from the butcher's in the village; free range, organic eggs from there too; mushrooms and tomatoes from the greengrocer's. The only thing she bought frozen was hash browns, because she couldn't be bothered with grating potato.

One thing that amused her was how quickly Finn and Dave had clocked that she was cooking breakfast in the morning when she had guests. They both often mysteriously appeared under some pretext or another, begging; their about-to-die-of-starvation faces firmly in place.

She clipped Rebus' lead on, and they were soon in Pennypot Lane. More snow had fallen overnight, and the lane looked magical, with virgin snow covering the squashed brown of yesterday's track and the foot marks on the tarmac. Today was a new day and the sun was streaming down on tree branches, creating fractals of light. It was just below freezing still, so nothing was going to melt today.

Under different circumstances, she'd be striding down the road cheerfully. Ordinarily, she loved being out this early with Rebus.

But Penelope Wyndham was dead, and it was obvious it was murder.

As she followed Rebus along the lane, her thoughts slid to Rebecca, Penelope's daughter, and the visit she'd paid them. The death, on its own, was going to be upsetting enough for her family and friends. But now, it seemed, there were estrangements, and Penelope's daughter was issuing threats...

Chapter 5

Ellie was out when Sylvia got downstairs just before 7am.

The B&B guests were up. She'd heard them in the shower.

She had a quick breakfast, moved Ellie's Yucca plant out of the kittens' reach and started gathering the ingredients for mince pies.

Unsalted butter. Mincemeat. Armagnac.

After a broken night's sleep and disturbing dreams about Penelope's body on the floor at Mistletoe Manor, she was keen to keep her mind occupied.

Caster sugar. Flour. Ground almonds.

She trebled her quantities so there would be plenty for the family and enough for the village bakery. It meant she'd need to hang around a bit while they were baking, but that was OK. She'd get the first batch in the oven and do her Wim Hof breathing. Zoe had introduced her to it, and she was hoping it might help soothe her nervous system after last night's shock.

Ten minutes later, Sylvia slid the first tray into the oven, then headed into the lounge before she got distracted.

She lay on the sofa on her back, selected the Wim Hof breathing track on her phone and played it through the speakers in the lounge

The music started and the man's familiar deep voice came on. *'This is a guided breathing.'* His Dutch accent. *'Help you relax to the deepest level.'*

The booming gong reverberated through the lounge. Sylvia rested her legs flat and closed her eyes.

'Are you ready? Round number one. Breathe in through your nose, out through your mouth. Follow the breath. In, out. In, out.'

It was fast.

'No pause between the in-breath and the out.'

Sylvia followed along.

'Like a wave. Circular.'

A volley of barks from Rebus alerted Sylvia to the arrival of a visitor at the door.

'In, out. Let go and follow my count.'

She was tempted to ignore the door and pretend no-one was in. But Rebus was now squealing, a sign he'd recognised whoever it was. She got up and ambled over to the door. Through the window to the right, she saw it was Dave.

'No pause between the inhalation and exhalation.'

She let him in. 'Morning.'

'Give it all you got.'

'What on earth is that?' Dave crouched down to give Rebus a fuss.

'I'll turn it off. It's...' She didn't bother explaining as she knew he would rib her about what he called her 'woo' interests.

'Well done. Into the belly.'

She reached for her phone and switched off the video. 'There we are.'

'I need to ask you few more questions about last night. Some things have come to light that we need to explore further.' He sniffed the air towards the kitchen in an exaggerated fashion.

'Sure. Come in.'

'Ellie about?'

Sylvia shook her head. 'She's probably gone to the high street.'

'We've got the carol service at the cathedral in Canterbury tomorrow evening,' Dave explained. 'I wanted to see if she fancied a bite to eat afterwards. I'll text her. We had to cancel last night because of Penelope's death.' He wrinkled his nose in a disappointed expression.

A few minutes later, they were sitting at the wooden table in the kitchen, a mug of coffee and a mince pie each.

'How did it come about that you were doing the catering for Penelope Wyndham?' he asked. 'Given the relationship between our family and hers, I wouldn't have thought you would be number one on her list of people to ask.' He moved Tallulah-the-tabby away from his mince pie for the second time.

Sylvia talked him through what had transpired, the same as she'd told Ellie and Zoe the night before. 'To be honest, it surprised me too. I wasn't in court when her husband was sentenced. I had no reason to be. But your dad was there, as it was his team which uncovered the evidence that clinched things.'

'Had you met her then, before you ran into her in the bakery? I mean, did she know that you're the wife of the detective who put her husband behind bars?'

'Oh, no doubt about that. We bumped into her one day in the supermarket. Your dad and I were doing a big shop before Easter and she was buying – I'll never forget – a tiny *poussin*, a pack of cranberry and onion stuffing and a half bottle champagne.'

'And she knew you were Dad's wife, did she? I mean, I know it's unlikely that he'd go shopping with a woman who *wasn't* his wife, but you could have been his sister.'

'Yes, your father introduced me. It was a bit odd, bumping into her in the frozen veg aisle, but that's village life for you.' She didn't need to say it was an occupational hazard of being a police officer. Dave knew only too well how often the professional collided with the personal. 'You know what a gentleman your father was. While I selected our *petit pois* and chips, he kindly asked her how she was and what her plans were for Easter.'

'What *were* her plans? Did she mention her family?' He bit into his mince pie.

Sylvia frowned as she tried to think back to their conversation several years ago. 'She didn't say very much at all. Just muttered that she was fine.'

'Oh, wow. These are delicious. Is that almond?'

'Yes. Frangipane on top of the mincemeat. Gives the fruit a lovely, rich, sweet flavour.'

Dave grunted through a mouthful, then spoke when he'd swallowed. 'And how was she towards you when you were at the manor house?'

Sylvia shrugged. 'Fine.'

'What did you talk about?'

'The food for the party... as you'd expect. Timings. Whether to use paper or real plates.'

'Nothing personal?'

'She made a bit of polite chat. Asked me about hobbies, that sort of thing.'

Dave nodded. 'OK. Now, going back to yesterday. You said you didn't see anybody at Mistletoe Manor. Presumably that means you didn't see anyone leaving as you arrived?'

'No.'

'No cars other than the stretch limo?'

'No.'

'No guests arriving early?'

She shook her head.

'You also said you checked the rooms upstairs. I want to be clear about this, so could you talk me through it again please?'

Sylvia did as he requested. She'd looked in four rooms in addition to Penelope's. No sign of occupation. A sixth room was locked. 'Actually, as I say all that, it's got me thinking. I didn't see any of the chauffeur's belongings in any of those rooms. Was he living there or does he have a house in the village?'

'It's our understanding he lived at the manor house. He's been the Selby's chauffeur for years. Practically one of the family.'

'In a "servant and master" kind of way,' Sylvia added. 'Who does the stretch limo belong to, then?'

'The Selbys. Did you see any keys? When you were in the kitchen or in the hall?'

'Not that I noticed, but I wasn't looking for *things*. I was looking for Penelope and Hargrave.' Sylvia couldn't help wondering where Dave was going with his line of questioning. There was obviously something going on with the chauffeur. 'Where is Hargrave?'

'I can't answer that. You know the score.'

An idea popped into Sylvia's mind. 'You know the notepad on the floor? Under her shopping list. It had "L" written on it.'

Dave's eyebrows went up. 'I can't discuss that either, I'm afraid.' He paused. 'Moving on – did she tell you why she rented Mistletoe Manor? Why *that* particular house, and why did she want to spend Christmas *here,* in Lower Wootton? One might think that, after all the bother with her husband's arrest, this would be the last place she'd want to move back to.'

'She didn't really say all that much. Just vague statements about "always loving it here," and being "pleased to be back home".'

'Hmm.' Dave nodded and Sylvia wondered what he was thinking about. 'What about her husband? Was she expecting him to join her for Christmas? And any other family?'

'Not that I remember her saying and I didn't ask. It was awkward. I didn't want to mention her husband and have her go on about the police, or the trial or his sentence.' She needed to tell Dave about the surprise visit from Rebecca. 'I do have some information about her family, though.'

She filled him in about the young woman who'd turned up the night before.

'*Rebecca?*'

'Yes. Penelope's daughter.'

Dave's face clouded. 'She doesn't have a daughter.'

'What?'

'Nope. No daughters. Just one son.'

Chapter 6

As soon as Dave left, Sylvia rang Ellie. The call went straight to voicemail, so she left a message telling her that Penelope had a son but no daughter.

Dave's information had sent her thoughts spiralling. Who, then, was the woman in the Parka who'd come round the night before, calling herself Rebecca? Why had she lied about her identity; why was she trying to find out about what had happened, and why had she warned them not to investigate? Or, as she'd put it, poke around in her mother's death.

The questions sent a shudder over her. It was bad enough that poor Penelope had been murdered. Now there was someone in the area masquerading as her daughter, trying to obtain information on false pretences. It was most unpleasant.

Then there was Hargrave. Could he have killed the woman he had been driving for?

Sylvia needed some fresh air and nature to calm her down. A wander around in the cold and snow in the garden would hopefully reset her brain.

She pulled on a jacket and wellies and left the animals in the house, making her way outside. The flower beds looked pretty, shrouded in snow. Off-white fairy lights twinkled on the Norwegian pine tree that Sarge and his nephew had planted the Christmas before last. They cast a warm light on the garden studio and surrounding snow.

There were large areas of snow-covered grass with no paw prints on it. Just an expanse of white crystals which glimmered in the weak winter sun.

In the outhouse, a light caught her attention. One of them must have left it on the night before, and it would be wasting electricity.

She trudged through the snow along the path to the wooden building. It was where she did her Joe Wicks workouts in the warmer months, but it was a bit cold in the winter. Although it was insulated, Ellie had decided not to install any heating.

She opened the door and a pungent smell hit her nostrils. Before she knew what was happening, a brown animal dashed past her and out into the garden.

'Whoa. What on earth?'

A figure moved on the sofa. Dark clothes, hoodie and padded waistcoat. It was Zoe in her work clothes.

'The gate,' Zoe yelled, as she scrambled to her feet. 'Make sure the gate's shut.'

Sylvia spun round to see what had passed her. A small, brown deer, with white spots and gangly legs, was leaping around in the garden. 'It's OK. It's shut. She's safe.'

'I picked her up last night just after midnight,' said Zoe. 'Terrified, by the side of the road. We think she might have had a near miss with a car and her family ran off. The refuge was closed so I brought her back here.' She checked her watch. 'Oh, darn it. I must have slept through my alarm. I'll ring now, see if someone can come and pick us up, take us back to the refuge.'

As she fished her phone out of her pocket and dialled, Sylvia heard a voice behind them.

'Um... Hi again.' It was Bridget in a pristine, waxed Barbour jacket and black Hunter wellies. 'We were up early and have pigged out on cereal and toast and coffee, and are full. We're going to–' She broke off. 'Um... Is that a deer in your garden or am I hallucinating?'

'It is. Sorry – excuse me,' said Zoe as she shimmied past the B&B guest.

'My granddaughter works at a wildlife rescue charity,' Sylvia explained, before realising Bridget had probably got the gist last night when the fox was mentioned. Hopefully, their guests wouldn't be too freaked out by the latest strange occurrence in their holiday let. They'd certainly have interesting stories to recount when they got home: someone murdered in the village on their first night. The body found by one of their hosts. Then a deer in the garden the following morning.

'Wildlife rescue?' Bridget followed Zoe outside. 'How exciting,' she said eagerly. 'I've only ever seen deer on the TV.'

'She's had a fright,' Zoe told them. 'Might need to wait for her to decide to come back inside the outhouse. I've got some pellets.'

'Sorry – I didn't finish what I was saying,' Bridget told Sylvia apologetically. 'Could you let Ellie know we don't need any more breakfast? Saves her cooking when she gets back.'

'Will do. Thanks for letting us know. I'll pass the message on.' She turned to Zoe. 'I'm going in. It's much too cold.' She pulled her jacket round her more thoroughly.

When Sylvia was back in the windmill, she sent Ellie a text about breakfast and fetched the office laptop. She started up Google and entered 'Penelope Wyndham' into the search bar, producing masses of results from all over the world. She added 'author' to the search term and quickly saw a website called *thepenelopewyndhamauthor.com*.

She clicked on the link and began scrolling.

When they were investigating, research was usually Zoe's role, but they hadn't made that decision yet, and Zoe was busy with the deer. Besides, Sylvia was perfectly capable. Ever since last night, she had been aware of a creeping curiosity about Penelope, combined with a sense of responsibility because she'd been the one who'd found her body. The others had said this feeling was misplaced, but she couldn't shift it. There was perhaps another element to it, too. Did she also detect a smattering of guilt? Penelope had clearly been affected by her husband going to prison. None of it was Sylvia's fault. Penelope's husband had made his own choices, and they were nothing to do with Penelope, as far as she knew. The news reports at the time hadn't mentioned any involvement on Penelope's part, had they? Not that Sylvia remembered. Similarly, *she* wasn't responsible for the arrests Ron made in his role as a detective.

Nevertheless, Sylvia knew what her feelings meant: she wanted to investigate the circumstances of Penelope's death. She would have a chat with Ellie and Zoe as soon as possible. In the meantime, she'd make a start by finding out about Penelope Wyndham.

The first thing Sylvia noticed on Penelope's website was the announcement in huge capital letters:

DUE TO PUBLIC DEMAND
HARRIET BLY WILL BE BACK
IN A NEW ADVENTURE,
COMING THIS CHRISTMAS!

Below this was a book cover. Bright colours, like the books she'd seen on the table in the Great Hall last night.

Sylvia scrolled down, slightly mystified. Hadn't Penelope retired a few years earlier? Wasn't 'due to public demand' a thing people said to drum up interest and excitement? And you never really knew whether it was genuine or not. She'd seen the exact same expression used recently. Now where was it? Ah, yes. The wool shop. They'd decided to reinstate their knit-and-natter group on Tuesday evenings. But the enthusiasm there was most definitely genuine. The ladies in the group had been devastated when it came to an end.

This was different. Who would demand a new book from a retired author and how would they make that demand? Who to? It sounded more like a marketing ploy.

She read a bit more.

'After an illness which left Penelope bedbound for nearly two years, and then undergoing medical treatment in the USA, she is now enjoying good health and renewed vitality. This means she is eager for new horizons and challenges.'

Hmm. She wasn't knocking Penelope's decision to start writing again, or minimising the effort involved in writing a book. It was simply that resurrecting her children's books didn't seem like a new horizon and challenge. Surely it was more like returning to an old one?

She read on.

More about her new book; her publisher. Sylvia clicked on the 'About' page.

'Penelope Wyndham is the award-winning author of the Harriet Bly children's adventure books.'

Yes, she knew that.

'Settled on the south coast of England in a manor house her main character would be proud of.'

Had she intended the move back to Lower Wootton to be a permanent one, then?

She wasn't really sure what she was looking for. She'd keep Googling, seeing what else came up. Next, she tried newspaper articles, skimming headlines.

Children's author retires.

Children's author flies to America for medical treatment.

Penelope Wyndham's husband is sentenced to eight years in prison for art fraud.

Son of children's author sets up wellness brand in wake of mother's illness.

That confirmed she had a son. They'd need to look into him, along with Penelope's husband.

But it was Rebecca who was intriguing her.

She googled 'Penelope Wyndham daughter'. Nothing came up. That was pretty definitive. She googled 'Rebecca Wyndham' and was shown a list of Facebook profiles which she clicked on and scanned, stopping when she saw a profile photo that was familiar…

It was the young woman who'd been round to the windmill last night. She had definitely said she was Penelope's daughter, not her daughter-in-law.

'Well, I never. Who are you, Rebecca Wyndham?' she asked the image and profile.

So, this woman wasn't just pretending to be Penelope's daughter. She'd even gone as far as setting up a Facebook profile in her name.

Chapter 7

'Why have I just seen a Kent Wildlife truck leaving here?' Ellie shouted upstairs when she got back from her walk. 'Please tell me Zoe hasn't brought *another* creature home?'

She unclipped Rebus' lead and hung it up; kicked off her boots and put her coat on a hook. With a bitter north-easterly wind outside, she was pleased to be back indoors in the warm.

'Yes and no,' came Sylvia's voice. 'Down in a minute.'

Ellie shuffled over to the worktop where the kittens were jabbing at drips from the tap with pudgy paws. Three batches of mince pies were on racks. 'Alright if I...?' She broke off, dispensing with asking permission and picked one up, inhaling its warm, sweet aroma. Mmm. Almonds and alcohol.

On the kettle lid, a Post-it note said, *'Don't forget carols tomorrow. Supper after? x'*

Her heart gave a flutter. She and Dave had been on a few dates over the last few months, and she'd enjoyed them, but she was frantically busy and kept having to change their plans. Hopefully, nothing would get in the way this time.

The B&B guests had left for the day and didn't need their cooked breakfast so she could crack on. Christmas was days away. She'd go through her list and prioritise what she needed to do.

She cleared the breakfast items from the table and settled herself there with a coffee.

'Zoe was doing a night shift and brought a young deer home,' Sylvia said, joining Ellie. She relayed the rest of the story.

Ellie rolled her eyes affectionately. 'Last time she put a fox in Rebus' crate. This house is becoming an animal sanctuary. Why can't she take these creatures to Finn's place, now that's her home? There's much more room there.' She pointed at the fresh cafetière. 'Got your message about Rebecca. That's very odd.'

Sylvia updated her on what she'd found on the internet about Penelope.

'Have you told Dave?'

Sylvia nodded. 'I'm sure his teams have found the information themselves though.'

'Where is the son? Do we know?' Ellie caught the concerned expression on Sylvia's face. 'When Felix and Penelope moved here, he must've already left home. I don't remember him being part of the village or anyone mentioning him.'

She told Ellie about the wellness business. 'Haven't got round to Googling him yet. Presumably the police will have been in touch with him.'

'What did Dave want?'

'He came round to ask me some questions. There's definitely something strange going on, Ells.'

Ellie waited to see what she was going to say, a hunch forming.

'You probably won't be surprised... but I'd like to investigate.'

The statement confirmed what Ellie had expected.

Sylvia's eyes filled with tears. She sniffed and rubbed her face, struggling to regain her composure. 'I should have gone back in the limo with Penelope after the lights. If I had done, she might not be dead.'

Ellie put her mug down. She would do what she could to make sure Sylvia didn't continue to feel guilty but, for now, she didn't want to interrupt her train of thought.

'It sounds like Hargrave the chauffeur has gone AWOL,' Sylvia went on. 'It could be a coincidence, but I can't help wondering if he might be implicated.'

'Hmm,' replied Ellie. 'I agree. It's strange behaviour.'

'And some woman is pretending to be the daughter Penelope never had,' Sylvia continued.

'Whatever has been going on with this Rebecca Wyndham woman was never going to go far once Penelope was dead,' Ellie countered. 'As soon as people became aware of someone claiming to be her daughter, she'd have been rumbled.'

'Yeah. But what has she been doing up 'til now? What if she's been blackmailing Penelope or embezzling money from her?' Sylvia's cheeks reddened with agitation and her eyes grew wider. 'She could be involved with Penelope's death – or not have anticipated it at all and now be annoyed her "cash cow" isn't going to be coughing up anymore.'

Sylvia had clearly been chewing things over and felt strongly about investigating, Ellie realised. But it was Christmas. Ellie had B&B guests booked solid for the next few months *and* she had agreed to host dinner for the family on Christmas Day. She wasn't keen on conducting another investigation at this point – but she could see a need was developing. If ever a case called for local knowledge, it was this one: there were so many people either 'missing in action', incognito, or of unknown whereabouts.

'I know the timing sucks,' said Sylvia, 'but poor Penelope has lost her life. I'm the first to admit I wasn't her biggest fan, but I'd really like to help her. See what we can turn up.'

Ellie found herself nodding. 'OK.' She explained how she felt. 'I'll text Zo. See when she can make a team meeting.' She tapped out a message and sent it. 'Tell me what Dave asked you. Any further clues as to what's going on?'

'It was mainly about why Penelope came back to the village.' Sylvia told Ellie about the information on author's website.

'"Settled at the manor house" suggests it was a permanent move,' said Ellie. 'I wonder why she didn't return to their marital home here?'

Sylvia shrugged.

'And why would she want to live in such a huge place?' Ellie continued. 'The rent and bills must be astronomical. I'd hate to live somewhere with so many empty rooms. It would make me feel lonely.'

'Yes, but that's how *you* would feel,' Sylvia told her. 'What we need to do is put ourselves in *her* position, *her* shoes. Imagine what she might have wanted. I don't wish to be needlessly mean but, let's face it, she's always been into image and status. Ron showed me the Wyndham's home once. Only from the bottom of the drive. It wasn't on the same sort of scale as Mistletoe Manor, but it's a detached farmhouse with acres of land. Must have at least six bedrooms.'

Ellie shuddered. 'All I can think about with a property that size is the dusting and vacuuming.'

'Says the woman who runs a cleaning business.'

'Exactly. That's because I know what it would involve. They usually have massive rooms for entertainment.

Grand Halls or something. Those rooms alone are usually the size of many people's flats.'

'You don't think she cleaned all those rooms herself, do you?' said Sylvia. 'She will have had *staff*, darling.' She said it with a flourish of her hand. 'A team of cleaners. Gardeners to cut all that grass in the summer and trim the hedges. In fact, the more I think about it, the more her decision to rent such a large property doesn't make sense.'

'I want to know what's happened to their marital home,' said Ellie. 'Do they still have it or has it been sold?'

'I don't know and, now you mention it, Penelope never brought it up. Perhaps her husband is living in it? It's something to find out. We'll need to track Felix Wyndham down and speak to him.' There was a determined glint in Sylvia's eye. 'Going back to the subject of Mistletoe Manor, while you were out with Reeby, I rang the number on the Selby's website for renting the property. Guess whose name Penelope's rental is in?'

Ellie shrugged. 'Why do I have a bad feeling about this?'

'Because you're a natural sleuth. Go on. Have a guess.'

'Hmm. Rebecca Wyndham?'

'Bingo.'

Chapter 8

'I've got half an hour tops, but I'll need a hot drink. My hands are freezing.' Zoe kicked her snowy boots off and bent down to give Rebus a hug. 'Ahem, Cleo.' Zoe swooped up the kitten, who was gnawing some shoelaces, and joined her mum and gran at the kitchen table. 'I've got to be in Worth by 11am to collect an otter that's been injured.' She was playing carols through the speaker on her phone.

On the table was a fresh pot of tea. Zoe put the kitten down and poured herself a mug. Rebus settled on the floor next to her chair.

'Let's get cracking then, if you're pushed for time,' said Ellie. 'Zoe, your gran wants us to investigate Penelope's death, and I've agreed. Are you up for it?'

Zoe's eyes lit up. 'I'm really busy at work. We've got four volunteers off because it's Christmas. But I'll help with whatever I can. I have to do quite a lot of hanging about, waiting for people and things. It's a good chance to get on the internet and research. I'm sure Sarge will give us a hand. Be right up his street.'

Ellie glanced at Sylvia. 'Why don't you fill us all in with what we know so far?'

'Sure. Having reflected on what Dave asked me earlier, and thought about my own concerns, questions are emerging about why Penelope returned to Lower Wootton to live, and why she chose Mistletoe Manor. Zo, lovey, you might not know all the details of the case involving Penelope's husband. It was around ten years ago, one of your granddad's last investigations before he retired. It culminated in Felix Wyndham going to prison for eight years for art fraud. The Wyndhams were living in Lower Wootton at the time.'

'Crikey. Was Penelope involved at all?' asked Zoe. 'Did she know what Felix was up to?'

'I don't know. That was kept quiet during the police investigation and as far as I'm aware, although I'm certain they questioned her, she was never arrested.'

'I'll do some digging,' Zoe replied, tapping herself a note in her phone.

'One of the things your dad asked me,' Sylvia continued, 'was whether Penelope knew I was Ron's wife.' She explained about having met her in the supermarket with Ron. 'Your dad also asked me how I came to be doing the catering for the reception that Penelope was hosting after the lights.'

'That's what *I* asked you too. Does Dad think that Penelope's death has something to do with you then, Gran?'

Sylvia shook her head. 'He wasn't able to confirm that.'

Ellie shuddered. 'He wouldn't have asked unless he thought it was relevant.'

'That's scary.' Zoe stared at her gran. 'Does that mean you could be in danger?'

Sylvia shrugged. 'The honest answer is – I have no idea. But it does make me wonder why Penelope wanted to come back and live here in the village when it's where her husband was arrested. She's hardly going to have lovely, fluffy memories of the place, is she?'

Zoe shrugged. 'Has she got family here in the village?'

'Not that I know of yet, but we still haven't located her son. He's not missing or anything – I simply haven't had time to look him up.'

'For the purposes of our investigation, what's important is that she *did* come back,' said Ellie, 'and, given her author website suggests the move was intended to be permanent, she clearly must've felt OK about it.'

'I'll take a look at her website later,' Zoe replied. 'Sorry, I'm catching up here. Let me Google the son. See what we can find.' She began jabbing at her phone screen.

'He's got some wellness brand.' Sylvia told Zoe about the headline she'd seen.

'Here we are. Zane Wyndham, forty-one. Runs Wyndham Wellness Ltd., registered to Beech Farm.'

'Isn't that the Wyndham family home?' said Sylvia.

'That's right,' Ellie replied.

Zoe continued. 'Zane set up the company when Penelope had meningitis. His website says: *"At Wyndham Wellness we passionately believe in the importance of viewing the whole person, not just an isolated symptom here and a test result there."*'

'Wow,' said Ellie.

'When my mother had meningitis, she was told she might never recover. We were determined to help her regain her health and her life. I've made it my mission to plough what we learnt during those dark days into the business, to help others.'

'I don't remember anyone mentioning the Wyndhams having children,' said Ellie. 'Maybe Zane went off to university and then started work. Does it say where he lives?'

'Not so far,' replied Zoe. 'Hang on. I've found another article in the *New York Times. "Being my mother's carer by Zane Wyndham".* Wow. He looked after her for two years while she was sick. Went over to the USA with her and everything.'

'Penelope wasn't living in the village then. She moved away when Felix went to prison. Only moved back very recently.'

'Poor Zane,' said Ellie. 'He must be devastated. I hope all his wellness training helps him to deal with his grief.'

'I'll keep looking for his address,' Zoe continued. 'Changing the subject, Gran, thinking about you doing Penelope's catering...'

'Uh-huh?'

'Did you get the impression your encounter in the bakery was complete chance, or set up to look that way?'

'Hmm,' replied Sylvia. 'I'm not sure. But even if Penelope set it up to look like she just bumped into me, that doesn't mean much. She might have felt awkward after Ron arrested her husband, I suppose.'

'It would make *me* feel awkward,' said Ellie. 'There's no way I'd want the wife of the man who put my husband inside doing catering for me. I wouldn't care how delicious her canapés were.'

'I agree it seems a bit unusual, but we don't know what her motivations were yet.'

Ellie was making a list in her notepad of the things Sylvia and Zoe mentioned.

'Moving on,' said Sylvia. 'We then have questions about the woman who came round last night.' She brought Zoe up to date about "Rebecca". 'I've sent her photo to your dad, although his digital teams will quickly find her profile, I'm sure.'

'I'll do some research on her too.' Zoe swiped her phone screen and was quickly on the internet. 'I've got to sit with a grey seal that's having a general anaesthetic later so I should have some time.'

Sylvia checked the clock on the kitchen wall. 'Then there are questions about Penelope's family. She has one son. Where is he? Was she expecting any family members to join her for the festive season? And, of course, where is her husband?'

'I take it he's been released from prison?' asked Zoe.

'A while back,' Sylvia replied. 'Eighteen months ago? Where he went after that, I've no idea. I'll see if I can dig around in the court documents. Find out what his probation terms were. He has to be a person of interest.'

Sylvia was an ex-social worker, and her experience and contacts invariably came in useful in their investigations.

'Gosh, this case involves such a lot we don't know.' Zoe helped herself to another mince pie.

'I've been thinking that too,' Sylvia agreed. 'Considering Penelope's family, we know Rebecca isn't Penelope's daughter, but I can't help remembering that she seemed to know things about the Wyndham family. Didn't she?'

'That's right,' said Ellie. 'She has to be a person of interest too. She said something about Penelope and Felix having an odd relationship. And she was clearly interested in where he was. I wonder why.'

'We need to find out who she is,' said Zoe. 'Is it illegal to impersonate another person?'

Sylvia shrugged. 'I suppose it depends on the purpose. I mean, technically, acting is impersonating someone with the purpose of entertainment.'

'I'll ask Dad. He doesn't need to tell me anything about the case to answer that.'

Sylvia gave her a thumbs-up. 'Lastly,' she said, 'Hargrave concerns me. Going AWOL is not the behaviour of an innocent man.'

'It definitely makes him seem sus,' agreed Zoe.

'I didn't see any sign of him at Mistletoe Manor,' Sylvia told them, 'and the four bedrooms I looked in didn't have any male-type belongings in them.' She reminded them of the one locked room.

Ellie jotted that down.

Sylvia continued, 'I'll have a think about anything Hargrave said to me, on the occasions I was there, which might provide a clue as to where he's from – or might be hiding out.'

'Someone round here will know who he is,' said Ellie. 'You know what the village is like.'

'Is Hargrave his first name or his surname?' Zoe asked. 'Is it even his *real* name?'

'That's a good point,' said Ellie.

'It's a very "chauffeur-y" sort of name,' Zoe added. 'Posh-sounding, like butlers' names in period dramas on TV.'

'So, we need to track down Felix and Penelope's son,' Ellie summarised, 'and Hargrave and Rebecca.'

'Ooh,' said Zoe. 'Before I forget, Gran, have you got the number there for whoever you rang to ask about Penelope's booking of Mistletoe Manor?'

Sylvia flicked through her notepad. 'Here we are. Mobile number. It was on the manor house's website. I spoke to a chap called Neville Selby.' She passed the notepad to Zoe who brought up *themistletoemanor.com* on her phone.

'Now this is interesting,' Zoe told them, studying the information on her screen. 'Under "Facilities", the Selbys mention the chauffeur-driven stretch limo and live-in chauffeur-come-housekeeper and say he's included as part of your stay.' She read aloud. *'Hargrave has driven for the Selby family for several decades, just as his father did before him.'*

'What was it you said about Penelope's notepad?' Zoe asked.

Sylvia told her about the 'L'.

'Can I see the picture you took of the note?' Zoe asked.

Sylvia rummaged about in her bag for her phone. 'It looked like Penelope was writing her shopping list and was interrupted. Who knows what the "L" might have been going to be.' She showed Zoe the photograph.

Zoe pursed her mouth in concentration. 'The "L" isn't directly under the last item on her list. If the killer came into the room, already aggressive and threatening, Penelope might have started writing a clue for the police and hastily stopped, then dropped the pad.'

'That sounds plausible,' replied Sylvia. 'She might've sensed danger before the killer made his full intention clear.' She glanced at her two fellow sleuths. 'It's worth bearing in mind anyway.'

'Do you think it was Hargrave?' asked Zoe.

'I think he needs to be a key suspect. His disappearance bothers me. People don't do that unless they've got something to hide, do they?'

Ellie tapped her chin. 'Sticking with Hargrave and his father, we've got two generations of chauffeurs. Someone in the village will know who they are. I'll mull over whose family has lived here for generations. Mine has, but I'm not asking Mum.'

Sylvia grunted at the mention of Ellie's mother. 'No. Please don't. The last thing we want is her turning up again, interfering.'

Zoe clicked on the number for the manor, putting the call on loudspeaker. It rang a few times, then:

'Neville Selby. How can I help you?'

'Ah, hello there, Mr Selby,' said Zoe, putting on a posh accent. 'My name is Ophelia Norton-Gray. I wanted to enquire about your beautiful home, Mistletoe Manor, on behalf of my grandmother, Lady Constance.'

'It won't be available for at least two weeks,' he replied matter-of-factly. 'We need to do some... er... *maintenance* on it. Would that suit?'

'Yes. That's the timeframe we're looking at. My grandmother has mobility issues. I see on your website it comes with a chauffeur. Could I check that's still current?'

The three women held each other's gaze.

'Er... It isn't, I'm afraid. Hargrave has... um... very sadly, had to leave us.'

'Oh dear. That's a shame. Nothing too concerning, I hope?'

Ellie elbowed Zoe. She was a cheeky mare.

'Er...'

In the background a woman whispered, 'Retirement.'

'He's had to retire,' Neville continued. 'Health issues, regrettably. But please tell your grandmother we will be replacing him for the next let once we've sorted a few... er... *practical issues.*'

Zoe mouthed 'eek' at her mum and gran, her face horrified.

'The limo will remain at the property,' Neville added.

'Thank you. That's good to know.'

Something had obviously happened with Hargrave.

'I'll have a chat with Grandmama and give you a call back. See how she feels. It looks a beautiful home.'

Chapter 9

After Blix Investigators' meeting, Zoe went back to work and Ellie and Sylvia started on their list of actions. The first was to go to the Wyndham's marital home and see who was living there now.

They crawled at 30mph round icy lanes on the outskirts of Lower Wootton. 'Thank goodness for snow tyres and four-wheel drive,' said Ellie. 'Are you sure it's this way?'

'Not one hundred per cent but keep going. There's nowhere to turn anyway.'

Pure, white snow covered the tarmac. It lay on the trees, bushes and verges.

'I've only been along here a few times,' said Ellie. 'As kids, there were rumours that the copse on the left was haunted by the ghost of a woman.'

'Oh?' said Sylvia. 'Not heard that one.'

'In my teens, I looked it up and discovered a woman had died of grief after her husband was shot down in WWII. I suspect the strange sights and sounds were a farmer with a rifle or a poacher.' Ellie changed the subject. 'What's the likelihood that Felix Wyndham is going to be there, do you think?'

'Hmm. Given Rebecca – I'm going to call her that until we find out her real name – didn't know where he was, I'd say it's got to be a pretty low chance, as it's an obvious place for her to have tried, surely?'

'That's a good point,' said Ellie. 'She must've been following the death closely as she knew I'd found Penelope's body. I can't figure out how she got that information.'

They drove a little further and had to pull in to allow a pickup truck to pass.

'That's Sarge's nephew,' said Sylvia.

As he pulled up alongside Ellie, she saw the new company sign he'd had installed on the outside of his vehicle. ROOTS & SHOOTS GARDENING. She wound her window down, getting a waft of cold, snowy air.

Sean lowered his window too. 'Morning.' He was a cheerful young man with a stocky build and a ginger beard.

'Love the livery. Very smart.'

'Thank you.' He grinned. 'Sarge suggested the name. Got my little brother working with me now. So, you'll see two of my vehicles driving around the area. Where are you ladies off to then?'

'Beech Farm.' An idea occurred to Ellie. 'Used to belong to Penelope and Felix Wyndham. And might still... we aren't sure.'

'Ah, the lady who's just died.'

'Yes. Do you know the property?'

'I do actually. Are you investigating her death?'

Ellie nodded.

Sean had always found their investigations exciting. Apparently, he often asked Sarge to find out what was going on.

'The owner used to have a gardener,' he said, 'but they sacked him. Nice chap. Someone contacted us a few months ago to see what our rates are, but was looking for someone to do a cheap job. Once I'd visited and told him how much it would cost to just cut all the grass, he got off the phone like a shot.'

'Did the person calling give a name?'

'Yeah. Zane.'

'That's the son. Did he give you his number?'

'He will have. I'll dig out my record of the call in my notebook. I log names and numbers in case they call back. We're getting so many new enquiries these days, I can't always remember who they're from otherwise.'

'And you went up to the farmhouse, you say?'

'Yes. Zane said he'd be away and to drive in and measure up.'

'Did you meet anyone?'

'Nope. Not a soul.'

'Did you get the impression anyone was living there at all?'

'Hard to tell. It's a massive place. Someone could be using a couple of rooms and you'd never know.' A black Labrador climbed onto Sean's lap and poked her head through the window.

'Hello Molly.'

'She's having puppies. Found out last week. So glad we've got our own place now.'

'Ahh.'

Sarge was going to miss his nephew. They'd lived together for years.

Sean smiled. 'People have already requested them. Anyway, I'd better get off. Customer's got a tree down in Ripple. I'm meeting the tree surgeon in ten minutes.' He pointed ahead. 'Beech Farm is another half a mile along this road, on the left. Big posh gates.'

They said goodbye and set off again, passing a five-bar gate with a robin sitting on it.

'This looks familiar,' said Sylvia. 'I remember that gate and the giant fir tree.'

They continued slowly. Under different circumstances, it would be a scenic and enjoyable drive.

An entrance was coming up.

'Here we are,' said Sylvia. 'I recognise the acorns and the pillars. This is it.'

'Should we park here and walk up, or drive?' asked Ellie.

'Well, we're here on legitimate business and want to speak to whoever's here. So, we don't need to sneak around. Let's drive up.'

They turned into the drive and were greeted with an expanse of snow-covered grass. Circular flower beds, containing wispy, naked bushes and crushed plants, lay beneath a white blanket; a branch poking out here, a leaf there. Bare trees rose from the ground. Under one, a wooden bench nestled, its slats covered in snow. The latest fall was untouched. Not a paw mark, tyre track or footprint.

'Wow. Wonder if anyone's at home?' asked Ellie.

'Let's find out.'

It was a sprawling property. The main building was covered with ivy at the front with four, large, panelled, sash windows either side of the front door, all with white shutters.

Sylvia read aloud from an old Rightmove listing Zoe had found and texted to them.

'Grade II listed... a fine example of Georgian architecture...' She paused. 'See, I said they were ones for status.' She returned to the listing. 'Drawing room... two inglenook fireplaces... six bedrooms, four with en-suite bathrooms.'

'Is that the most recent sale listing?' asked Ellie.

'That's a good question. Let me check the history.' Sylvia scrolled on her phone while Ellie drove. 'Here we are. Sold in 1980 for £960,000. Last sold in 1994 for £1.6 million.'

Ellie sucked in a breath. 'That must be what the Wyndhams bought it for, then. Not exactly pocket money, is it?'

'No. Ron said Felix had a gallery with small auction rooms attached, in Mayfair in London.'

'That makes sense. I doubt very much you'd be buying a house at that price on the earnings of a children's author alone.'

As they approached the house, it was difficult to tell if anyone was at home. It was daytime and therefore hard to see if any lights were on.

'Unless they park them round the back, I can't see any cars, can you?'

'I was just thinking that.'

It was a pretty building. Red brick with large windows. The distance between the ground and first floor was substantial, suggesting large rooms with high ceilings.

'C'mon. Let's see if anyone's here.'

Ellie nodded. She parked the jeep and they made their way up snowy steps to the front door.

She pressed the bell and they waited. But no one came, even after she tried again. 'Let's go round the back.'

They trundled through the snow, along the side of the house, past a double garage and a tennis court, and were soon in a rectangular yard.

'No footprints here either.'

'I guess if someone's in, they could be asleep or not well.'

They approached the back door and Ellie knocked there. But as she did, the door swung inwards on its hinges.

'It's open. That's odd.'

Sylvia was frowning.

'Hello?' Ellie shouted. 'Is anyone there? Zane? Felix?' She gripped the door with one hand and banged on it with the other, hoping it might at least attract someone's attention.

'What if they've got an alarm?' said Sylvia.

'We'll soon find out, won't we?'

'Yeah, but then we'll be caught trespassing.'

'I think it's very unlikely,' Ellie told her. 'If they had an alarm on, the back door would have set it off, surely? Anyway, we'll soon find out.' She stepped over the threshold with Sylvia following.

'Hello? Anyone in?' She felt daft, shouting the same thing over and over.

They were standing in a vast kitchen, the size of the whole of the downstairs of the windmill. Double Aga. Cabinets along three sides. A solid oak table and chairs in the middle. Flagstone floor.

'What have we got here?'

On the table was a small plate with crumbs and a knife on it. A wrap of butter sat next to a jar of blackcurrant jam and a mug.

Ellie placed her fingers on the mug. 'Still warm. Someone's been here very recently.' She strode over to the fridge and opened it. 'Yep. There's a couple of Tesco ready meals and a bag of salad. Someone's living or staying here.'

'Where are they then?'

'Out for a walk? Asleep?' She faced the doorway into the hall and shouted again. 'Is anyone there? It's Ellie and Sylvia Blix from the village. We just want to ask a few questions.'

'Ells, I don't feel comfortable going much further. We're in the dead of countryside here. They might have a gun. We might startle them.'

'Let's just see if there's any post. Something with a name on it that might tell us who's living here.' Ellie walked into the hall and approached a long sideboard which ran along the wall to a double-doored entrance with a porch. 'Here we are.' She'd spotted a bundle of paper and began shuffling through it. 'Newspaper. A wadge of post.' She grabbed up the envelopes and read out the names: 'Penelope Wyndham. Zane Wyndham. Wyndham Wellness Ltd. Felix Wyndham.'

'Looks like we've found two family members,' said Sylvia. 'Well – their post.'

'This isn't just junk mail either. Some of these look official. Zane's got his business correspondence coming here. And there's one for Felix, from Dover Council.'

Ellie had a look at each item, shuffling through. One for Penelope was from *Yacht World*. She knew what that was as her mother had once dallied with the idea of buying a yacht.

She held it up for Sylvia to see.

'Wow. I guess she could have been dreaming. I wonder why Felix and Zane are having post sent here?'

Ellie shrugged. 'Convenience? Perhaps this place is Felix's registered address?'

Sylvia started saying one of the names aloud. 'Zane Wyndham? *Zane Wyndham*. Now – where do I know that name from?'

'We've been talking about him quite a bit,' Ellie suggested.

'I mean well before that. I've heard his name mentioned somewhere and I can't for the life of me think where.'

'It'll come to you,' Ellie told her. 'Let's go back outside. Have a look round. See if anyone's out there.'

Barns, stables and outhouses ran off the yard. One barn was open at the front and various vehicles had been left here. An old combine harvester. A tractor. A crop sprayer. And at one side a Volkswagen Golf was parked. Navy blue with a 2009 plate.

Ellie took a snap of the registration. As private investigators, they didn't have the powers to check who owned it, but it might help them in case they saw the vehicle again.

'I don't know about you but I'm not getting a sense of wealth here, are you?' she said. 'That car's fifteen years old. Sean said Zane wanted the gardening done as cheaply as possible. The food in the fridge isn't from Waitrose or M&S. It's from Tesco.' She searched Sylvia's face.

'No. And if the Golf's Zane's, it's not exactly an example of an eco-car, is it?' Sylvia replied.

Ellie's phone buzzed in her pocket.

'Hmm. I suppose it could be his spare vehicle. Or someone else's. Or – he bought it before his conversion to wellness and hasn't traded it for an environmentally sound model.'

Sylvia shrugged. 'Sticking with money – do we know if the Wyndhams have financial problems? Penelope must've been doing OK, given she rented Mistletoe Manor. But where is Felix?'

They walked through an arch and arrived in another yard, this one smaller with a large barn which was open at the front. Ellie got a whiff of manure. Inside the barn, behind railings, a tall figure was moving and a bulky animal shot from one side to the other. A calf or a sheep?

'Ten scoops of pellets,' a male voice counted, 'five of beet... and another hay bale.'

'Think we've found Zane,' Ellie whispered, recognising him from the PR shot on his website, and wracking her brain for how they were going to explain being there.

She cleared her throat loudly, hoping that would alert him to their approach. 'Sorry to make you jump.'

He stopped moving hay.

She leaned over the railing. 'Are you Zane? We knocked at the door and came round.'

'That's me. And you are?' He had a pleasant face and glanced at Sylvia through mousey blonde dreadlocks which he pushed back, seeming to decide the two women weren't a threat.

Ellie introduced them and said, 'Really sorry about your mother.' She waited to see what he would say.

He tipped the dry feed into a trough, a muscle twitching in his bearded cheek.

Ellie counted four sheep.

'Thank you. I'm having trouble taking it in.' He picked up a hay bale and chucked it down for the animals. 'She was such a vibrant person, you know? Full of excitement about this new book she'd written. Thrilled to be back in the swing of it again and connecting with her readers.'

'You were in touch with her then?'

'Of course.' He covered his face with his hand, letting out a whimper. 'We've always been–' He broke off, wiping his eyes with his sleeves and seeming to gather his thoughts. 'We've always been close. When I was a kid, while my dad was busy working, Mum would take me to football training and swimming. And Dad, on the rare occasions he did take me, he'd drop me off and leave straightaway, whereas Mum would always stay and watch, cheer me on, you know? Take me for hot chocolate or ice cream afterwards. Maybe it was an only child thing. Whatever.' He gave a grief-stricken shrug. 'I felt really lucky.'

He frowned, as though he'd just realised he was talking to complete strangers. 'Sorry, who did you say you were again?'

Ellie and Sylvia exchanged glances.

Ellie re-introduced them.

'It was me who found your mother,' Sylvia told him.

'We were... a bit worried,' Ellie added, 'because no one seems to know where your father is.'

The police might have tracked him down, but they had no way of knowing.

Zane grunted.

Ellie wasn't sure whether to mention the visit from Rebecca.

'That doesn't surprise me one bit,' he replied. 'Dad's nickname with Mum and me was the Scarlet Pimpernel.' He brushed sheep feed off his hands. 'Look, it's cold out here. Shall we go inside?' He let himself out of the animal enclosure and secured the railings, then strode past Ellie and Sylvia. 'The sheep belong to the farm next door. The farmer's son usually comes over and feeds them, but I said I'd do it while I'm here.' He marched across the yard to the back door.

'Now's our opportunity to get some information', whispered Sylvia.

They followed Zane into the house, waiting inside the door and watching as he made a beeline for the Aga and switched the kettle on to boil.

'Is it just you living here?' asked Sylvia. 'Big old place.'

'Sort of. I don't live here though. I'm just staying here while...' He stopped mid-sentence. 'Can I get you ladies a cup of tea or coffee?' He had a kind manner.

'Not for me thank you,' Ellie replied, hoping he would elaborate on his family situation. Was he married? Did he have children? If he was only staying here, where was his home?

'Nor me, thanks.' Sylvia cleared her throat and in a gentle voice prompted, 'Have you had to come far?'

'My partner and I live in Sandwich with our children. I've never lived in the village. I'd left home when my parents bought Beech Farm. Met my wife at university and we moved to Sandwich.'

That confirmed what Ellie had been thinking. 'It's very close, isn't it?'

'Yes. That was part of it. We've always wanted to stay near Mum; make sure she's OK. Things weren't easy for her with Dad's trial and conviction. Nor when he was in prison. I was pleased when she moved from this place. Couldn't understand why she wanted to move back to Lower Wootton for Christmas. Especially renting that massive manor house.' He turned and faced Sylvia. 'But she said she wanted to treat herself. She's always liked her luxuries and has never been a fan of this place.'

Ellie nodded, hoping he'd carry on talking.

'Blix,' he said. 'From the village. I'm guessing you're related to Detective Inspector Ron Blix, then, are you?'

'He's my late husband.' Sylvia paused. 'We aren't here to cause any trouble. I was genuinely the person who found your mother and..'.

'Oh, it's OK, I know. The police told me.' He frowned. 'Are you the people who run the private investigators' business? I've read about you in the local rag.'

They were going to have to tell him the truth.

Ellie looked at Sylvia, waiting for her to explain. She was the one who wanted to investigate.

'Yes, although it's more of a labour of love than a business,' Sylvia told him. 'We don't charge people. We – that's Ellie, plus my granddaughter and I – conduct private investigations for people in the village. They're either people we know or they're situations that seem suspicious. I've been telling my daughter-in-law I felt guilty because I was going to go back to Mistletoe Manor in the limo with your mother after the light switching-on ceremony, but I changed my mind and decided to walk.'

Zane's features were scrunched as he listened to Sylvia, as though he was struggling to take it in.

'I can't help thinking that, had I stuck to the plan, things might have been different.'

He gave her a faint smile. 'I'm sure there's no need for you to feel bad, Mrs Blix. Mum will have had Hargrave with her.'

'Thank you. That's very generous of you. I... we would like to help, though. Of course, the police are conducting their investigation, but we would be happy to dig around, see what we can find out. Use our local knowledge...'

Zane leant back on the wall, pausing briefly to check on the stove. 'If you've got the time, that would be very kind. Thank you.' He was shaking his head in disbelief. 'Anything that helps find out who did this to Mum.'

'In the past our investigations have been very successful. My son's the–'

'Ah. The detective who came round last night. Yes, that makes sense now.' He shuffled over to the oak table and picked up the mug that was there. Took it over to the sink, gave it a swill out and placed it on the worktop.

He was a tall man, taller than Dave, so that would put him at around six foot three. Ellie noticed a slight limp. He reminded her of a Saluki dog.

'Do you know anyone called Rebecca?' asked Sylvia.

Zane turned, frowning. 'I've got a Rebecca in my PR team. Is that who you mean?'

Sylvia explained about the woman who'd visited them.

'She definitely said her name was Rebecca?'

'Yes. It was rather peculiar. She asked if we knew where your dad was and told us not to investigate your mother's death.'

'That doesn't make sense.' He paced across the room. 'So, this person is asking questions about Dad and issuing warnings on the family's behalf?'

It took Zane a few minutes to make himself a cup of tea and sit down at the kitchen table.

Ellie brought up the fake Facebook profile on her phone screen and, while Zane was looking at something else, she held it up for Sylvia to see, raising her eyebrows questioningly.

Sylvia nodded.

'There's more, unfortunately.'

He looked up first at Ellie then Sylvia.

Ellie passed him her phone.

'What's this?' He took it and examined the image.

'Whoever she is, she's got a Facebook account,' Ellie replied.

He leant forward in his chair, resting his elbows on his knees, studying Rebecca's picture. 'This is getting weirder and weirder. I have no idea who this is. I wonder what they want.' He screenshotted the image with his own phone.

'We've sent details of the Facebook account to the police so their digital teams should be able to establish who created it. My daughter, Zoe, is going to do a reverse image search and see what comes up. We'll let you know.'

He nodded. 'Thank you. I usually get one of the girls to show me how to do most tech-type stuff. They're so much more adept.'

'I'm older than you and rely on my granddaughter for the same thing. It's all apps these days.' Sylvia smiled. 'While we're here, is it OK to ask you a few questions about your mother? It'll save us coming back and hopefully means we'll be able to get cracking as soon as we leave.'

'Sure.' He sat back in his seat and handed Ellie's phone back. 'What would you like to know?'

'Before your mother died, was anybody causing her stress? Had she had any fallings-out? Any long-term feuds? Sorry. I know they are upsetting things to think about.'

'It's fine. The police were asking me these questions, so I'll tell you what I told them.' His voice took on a tone of drudgery, as though he'd told the tale numerous times already and found it utterly draining. 'Mum and Dad weren't on good terms. They haven't been for years. In fact, she was on the verge of leaving him a number of times and he always persuaded her to stay. Promised he'd mend his ways, be nicer, be around more, be a better husband.'

He shrugged. ‘But – he *never* kept his promises. Often, when they had arguments, he’d turn things round and say he’d be much better off without her. That *he* was leaving *her*.’

Ellie listened, aware of the pain behind his words.

‘Did you get any indication that he felt strongly enough to think about killing her?’

‘Oh yes. He regularly threatened to kill her.’

Ellie gasped and glanced at Sylvia.

Zane shook his head. 'I know. It was shocking.'

'Must've been upsetting and frightening for you as well,' said Ellie. She collected her thoughts. ‘Sorry to ask further about this. We appreciate it’s sensitive. We need to be clear about your dad’s feelings and motivations towards your mother. Do you know what the issue was? What had your mother done that annoyed him so much?’

‘This is the thing. Nothing. I think he’d simply fallen out of love with her or found other interests. It would’ve been much better if they’d split up, but neither of them seemed to be able to make the break.’ He gave a perplexed, sad shrug. ‘They’d been together a long time. I suppose they both had their reasons.’

It was a story Ellie had heard before. All too human. People were unhappy in their relationship but also didn't want to leave. Was it fear of being alone? Of starting again? Exhaustion, sometimes?

'Did she report the threats to the police?'

'I'm not sure. I kept telling her to, so that it was documented in case something like this happened.'

Ellie caught Sylvia's eye.

'Do you think he'd be capable of doing this? *Of killing her?*'

'Oh, yes,' he replied, his voice grave. 'I do. The police told me Mum was strangled with some fairy lights. And–' He broke off with a sob. 'The thing is, he's tried before. Many years ago, when I was growing up.'

'With fairy lights?'

'Yes. I burst in on them. Dad had the cord round her neck.'

'That must've been terrifying,' said Ellie. It had to make Felix their number one suspect. 'Did you tell the police all this?'

He nodded.

'Are you in touch with your father?'

'Only vaguely. I have an old mobile number for him. I can give you that if you like? I only ever hear from him when he wants something.'

'So, you don't know where he's been living since he left prison?'

'Afraid not.'

'Do he and your mother own this place jointly?'

'I don't know. Mum was trying to find out from Dad's solicitor, but he wouldn't tell her. My wife checked the Land Registry for her and the listing was being updated. Apparently, it can take ages.' He rolled his eyes. 'I'm not very technical... and Mum? She could barely manage to operate the alarm system here. Left it off most of the time.'

Ellie glanced at Zane's phone on the table. It was an old model, battered and with a cracked screen. She was always curious when someone wasn't plugged into the world's tech-crazy systems. 'I gather you run a wellbeing business. What's that?'

'We specialise in helping people to view themselves holistically. That way they can simplify their lives and down-regulate their nervous system.'

'Ah.' Ellie had no idea what 'down-regulate their nervous system' meant. It sounded a bit new-age.

'Hence the crappy phone,' Zane added.

Ellie changed the subject back to Penelope's estate. 'Do you know who your mother's heir was? Did she make a will?'

Surprise stretched over Zane's features. 'I never thought to ask her and I haven't heard anything. But I'm certain Dad will have made sure he was her heir. There's no way he'd risk losing everything. He's much too calculating.'

If his mother had left a will, and Zane was in it, he would be contacted by the executor.

Sylvia ambled over to an exposed brick wall, where three framed landscape paintings hung. They were by a local artist, Denis Hamilton. Huge canvasses. Seascapes. White, chalk cliffs. Open fields.

She gestured to the wall. 'Was this what your father liked?'

He snorted contemptuously. 'He liked whatever made him the most money.'

'What did your mother know about your father's art fraud?'

'Nothing at all. It was a complete shock when the police told her what he'd been up to. His main gallery was in London. He rented a tiny space in Canterbury, but spent most of his time in Mayfair and had most of his collection there. We gather he organised all the fraud from there.' He sighed. 'Poor Mum. She was horrified by the whole thing. Had the media outside the house here for weeks, ambushing her as soon as she set foot out of the door, firing questions at her, shoving their lenses in her face.'

'It must've been a very difficult time,' said Sylvia.

'We'll follow up on your father,' said Ellie. 'Again, sorry to pursue this.' She fished her phone out of her pocket, aware it had been vibrating at intervals. 'Were there any other people not kindly disposed to your mum?'

He shook his head mournfully. 'Not that I can think of. Apart from Dad – everyone loved her.'

Ellie and Sylvia left Zane. As they were walking towards the jeep, Ellie swiped her screen. Several missed calls and a message alert. She dialled into her voicemail.

'Sorry to bother you. It's Bridget. We... er... we've locked ourselves out.'

Ellie groaned.

'Don't suppose you could let us in, could you?'

Chapter 10

Ellie and Sylvia had just left Beech Farm and were walking back to the jeep. The snow had finally stopped but there was a bitter wind.

'Can't the guests use the spare from the key safe?' asked Sylvia. 'Isn't that what you had it installed for?'

'Yes, but Dave borrowed it last weekend and forgot to put it back.'

Sylvia rolled her eyes. 'That was useful.'

'We're heading back to the windmill anyway,' Ellie told her. 'I've asked them to wait for us. The pub's open so they won't be standing in the snow.'

As soon as they got in the jeep, Ellie's phone rang through the Bluetooth system. It was Zoe.

'Hey Mum. Just found out something interesting about Penelope Wyndham. A few years ago, another children's author accused her of stealing their work.'

'Oh?'

'Local guy called Toby. Lives in Ripple. He'd done a course with Penelope. Apparently, the fee included some mentoring. Penelope read students' work and gave them feedback. Toby alleged that his story contained something particular in it. Eighteen months later, this particular story element appeared in Penelope's next book.'

'Oh, wow. That sounds messy. What happened?'

'There were public exchanges on social media. Then he instructed a lawyer and things went quiet. However, gossip continued on the publishing grapevine and, rumour has it, someone put the frighteners on him.'

'All sounds very nasty. Were any names mentioned?' The first person who popped into Ellie's mind was Felix. Attempting to strangle Penelope. Threatening to kill her. Just the sort of person to try and intimidate someone making inconvenient allegations.

'I've managed to find a couple of threads on Reddit.'

'What on earth is Reddit?' asked Sylvia.

'A discussion forum on the internet. Still public but a bit more underground than a blog post. I'll have a further read later. I was doing it while I was waiting for a lady to get home so we could do a check on a fox in her garden.'

'That's a good find. Well done. How's the fox?'

'Fine, thankfully. It was a false alarm. The vet reckons he'd eaten too much and fallen asleep under a bush.'

'Have you got any contact details for Toby, lovey?' Sylvia shouted into Ellie's phone.

'Yep,' Zoe replied. 'He still lives in Ripple. I'll ping the details over now. Works in an independent record shop in Deal high street.'

'Is he still writing? Do we know how the disagreement with Penelope affected his career?'

'He wrote an article not long after things went officially silent, saying his agent had dropped him and prospective new agents wouldn't give him the time of day. He tried approaching a few publishers direct, but they also weren't interested in working with him.'

'Hmm. Could be a coincidence. Anyway – we definitely need to interview him. No-one instructs lawyers lightly; not least because their fees can run high. It sounds like he felt strongly about this stealing allegation. It might have given him a motive for wanting to harm Penelope. What's his surname?'

'Let me see. Toby...?' There was silence for a few moments while Zoe searched for the name. 'Here we are: Drysdale.'

'I'd say we need to add Toby Drysdale to our list of suspects. In joint place at number *two* with Hargrave – behind Felix.'

Chapter 11

On the way back to the windmill, Ellie and Sylvia discussed Zane Wyndham.

'Seems very pleasant,' said Sylvia. 'Obviously devoted to his mum.'

'I agree.'

They moved onto the possibility that Toby Drysdale might have been involved with Penelope's death.

'We'll need to interview Felix as soon as we can locate him,' said Ellie. 'And Toby. I'll get Zoe to come to the shop with me. She can talk music and records with him.'

When they turned into the drive, Sarge was waiting for them in the doorway, his shoulders hunched, and a worried frown furled across his face. Rebus sat next to him, a protective presence.

'Oh dear,' Ellie muttered. 'That's not a happy chappy. Don't tell me there's more bad news.'

'At least your guests will be in the warm,' Sylvia added begrudgingly.

They got out of the jeep. Ellie was wondering what on earth Sarge was waiting to tell them.

'I went to fetch my wellies from the outhouse,' he explained in his soft voice, 'and nearly passed out from the smell. I hate to tell you, but I think you've got an animal living in there. It stinks to high heaven and there were droppings everywhere.'

Ellie placed a reassuring hand on his arm. 'It's OK.' She explained about Zoe and the fawn. 'She's assured me she'll clean up this evening.'

'I've already done it,' he said. 'Couldn't leave it like that for you to walk into.'

'*I* walked into it this morning,' Sylvia said gruffly. 'Nearly got knocked off my feet by the deer as it dashed past me, too.'

Sarge smiled.

'That's very kind of you,' Ellie told him. 'I'm sure she'll appreciate having one less thing to do when she's finished work. The hours are one of the things I worry about with this new job of hers. I do hope she won't get too tired. Last time that happened she ended up with glandular fever.'

'Don't you worry about that young lady. She's a couple of years older now. Wiser. More resilient. She'll be fine. Takes after her mother, she does... Before I forget, Dave was round while you were out. Looking for you. Something to do with the carol concert?'

'Thanks. I'll give him a ring. While you're here, do you fancy a cuppa? I wanted to pick your brains on Penelope and Felix Wyndham, and Beech Farm.'

Sarge's eyebrows shot up and he snorted. 'That's going to cost you more than a cup of tea. At the very least it's going to take one of Sylvia's delicious frangipane mince pies. The bakers have run out already.'

Ellie gave him a knowing smile. She told him they'd bumped into Sean while they were in the lanes. 'Two liveried pickup trucks? Glad he's doing well now.'

They chatted briefly about Sarge's nephew.

Sylvia took Rebus in.

'Where would you like to start with the Wyndhams?' Sarge asked.

Ellie gathered her thoughts as they meandered up the path. 'Felix? Do you know him?'

'A little. When I was working at the garden centre, he asked me to help him with a number of trees and plants at Beech Farm. I suspect he asked me, rather than hiring a qualified horticulturalist, because he wanted to save money, which I found rather offensive; so I told him he would either have to pay me or make a receipted donation to a charity of my choice. Of course, he chose the latter. Probably managed to find a way to put it down to expenses of some sort.'

Ellie shut the door behind them. 'When did you last see him?'

'Two weeks ago. Wearing that awful trilby hat of his. He was sneaking around the village, behaving suspiciously.'

At least that was confirmation he was still alive and back in the area. Ellie had been starting to wonder.

'Oh? What was he doing that seemed suspicious?'

'He was knocking on doors and peering into people's gardens. I think he was looking for someone.'

'We've spoken to Penelope's son, Zane. He doesn't know where Felix is. Don't suppose you've heard anything?'

'I've no idea, I'm afraid. I had no desire to talk to him and made sure that didn't happen. He was around for a few days, though, so he must have been staying somewhere close by.'

Ellie caught sight of the vacuum cleaner, mop and bucket that were by the back door.

'Thanks for doing such a thorough clean-up in the outhouse. Hope doing it hasn't aggravated your back?'

Sarge had been a circus performer and had sustained a serious back injury when two trapeze artists had fallen on him.

'No, it's fine. I've just had a cortisone injection. Sean suggested it. Given me a new lease of life, it has.'

'That's good news. Could Felix have been lodging with Penelope at Mistletoe Manor?'

'I very much doubt it. I'm sure Zane put you in the picture about their relationship. Cordial, it was *not*. There was a lot of talk about their marriage. Several people said they feared one of them was going to end up dead.'

Ellie digested his comment. She knew people gossiped about other people's relationships and made jokey comments. But it wasn't often they said someone might end up dead.

'Zane said his mother didn't know who owned Beech Farm. I don't suppose Felix mentioned that to you when you were discussing the grounds?'

Sarge pursed his lips, as though he was casting back through exchanges with Felix. 'Not directly. I got the impression money was tight, and he said something about having to convince Penelope to agree to sell the place.'

'Really?'

'Yes. Could just be a figure of speech but that *might* suggest they co-owned it, don't you think? If the deeds were in his name only, he could simply sell it without asking her, if he wanted to. I could see he was ruthless.'

Could Felix have killed Penelope to get his hands on the farmhouse? It was a horrible thought.

'Overheard one of his phone conversations one day,' Sarge continued, 'and couldn't believe the way he spoke to whoever was on the other end. Swearing. Threatening. Impatient. If he hadn't had an Arran whitebeam on the estate, I would never have agreed to help him.'

'An Arran *what*?'

'Arran whitebeam. It's one of the rarest trees in the world. Someone's ancestor had it brought down from the Isle of Arran.'

'Interesting.' A feeling of dread crept over Ellie. 'I wonder who Penelope's heir was? Zane said he didn't know that either.'

'Yeah, but he's away with the fairies, that one,' replied Sarge. 'Nice enough, but "Wellbeing Consultant" indeed! Never heard such a load of mumbo-jumbo.'

Ellie chuckled at his dismissiveness. They adored Sarge. You never knew what he was going to come out with from one moment to the next. 'Apart from you not liking his job–'

'*Job?* It's not a job.' He grunted disapprovingly.

'OK, so apart from you not liking how he earns a living, he's a sound bloke though, right?'

'Oh, yes. And was a good son. Clashed with his father though.'

Ellie nodded. Zane had told them that. 'Changing the subject slightly, do you know the chauffeur at Mistletoe Manor?'

'Hargrave? Yes – very well. We used to go to youth club together in Deal. One down by the Recycling Centre in West Road. That's where I first learnt about the circus. I'm a bit older than him. Did you know the Selbys loaned

Hargrave to the Wyndhams when they didn't need him at Mistletoe Manor?'

'No-o. Really?' She'd never heard of families sharing a chauffeur. And the Selbys made a big thing on their website of Hargrave, and his father, having been part of their family for decades.

'Yes. So, there are links between the two families: the Selbys and the Wyndhams. Well, perhaps not families. More like between Neville and Felix.'

Sarge was nodding. He was such an interesting man. Ellie would've loved to have been a fly on the wall when he was growing up, and when he was working at the circus. She'd always got the impression he'd seen a lot of things.

'Was Hargrave around at all when you went to see Felix at Beech Farm?'

'Oh yes.' He chuckled. 'Hargrave is always around.'

'Except he somehow *wasn't* when Penelope was strangled. And now seems to have gone AWOL.'

'You're kidding?'

'Nope. When did you see him last?'

'At the lights switch-on in the high street when he was driving Penelope. Only in the distance to wave to.'

'Does he still have family round here?'

'I think so. When he was growing up, they lived in Fairfax Road in Sholden. Two roads away from our house. A couple of minutes' dash along the alley and over the fence.' He chuckled.

'Is Hargrave his real name?'

'No,' he said dismissively. 'His real name is Greg Wood. His old man used to drive for the Selbys too. We made up the name "Hargrave" for him. Heard it on the telly. We thought it sounded posh. When his dad retired, and Greg took over the job, he acquired the name his dad had been using.'

That confirmed what Zoe had learnt about father and son being the Selby's chauffeurs.

'Why d'you think he's disappeared?'

Sarge's face clouded over. 'I don't know and I don't like it.' He was shaking his head. 'It'll be for a good reason, mind. You mark my words.'

Ellie caught the concern in Sarge's voice. 'Did you know Penelope too or just Felix?'

'Other than seeing her around the village since she moved back here, I've never met Mrs Wyndham. Felix always made sure he invited me up when she wasn't going to be there.'

Chapter 12

Sylvia, Ellie and Zoe were in the kitchen discussing the Wyndhams.

'I can think of someone who might know about Felix and Penelope,' Sylvia told them.

She dialled Leonard's number, putting the call on loudspeaker.

'He's lived round here since the eighties. He knows everyone.'

Leonard answered. 'I was just thinking about you, my dearest fluffy lamb-y-kin.' His voice was thick with emotion.

Coke spurted from Zoe's mouth, spraying brown liquid all over the kitchen floor. '*Fluffy lamb-y-kin?*' She screamed with laughter, bringing Rebus bounding over, tail wagging.

Ellie nudged her with her elbow.

Sylvia flicked the loudspeaker off, giving them both an embarrassed look.

Zoe made a 'baa' noise and started jumping about, imitating a spring lamb.

'Sorry,' Sylvia said. 'With all the creatures she brings home, and the constant sound effects, it's like living in a menagerie.' She let out a faux-wearisome sigh. 'Anyway, the reason I was calling was to ask you about Penelope and Felix Wyndham.' She shot Zoe a dirty look. 'I'm going to put you back on loudspeaker, Leonard. OK?'

Ellie grabbed hold of Zoe and gently put her hand over her daughter's mouth.

'I married them, you know,' Leonard told them. Fortunately, he didn't appear to realise he'd just been on speaker. 'In 1992. Lovely church wedding with organ pieces by Wagner and Mendelssohn, if I'm not mistaken.'

'Do you happen to remember who their best man and bridesmaid were?'

'Now, let me think. The best man is easy. That was Leo Jones, Sally's father.'

Sally was Ellie's best friend.

'Penelope had two bridesmaids. One wasn't from here. She lived in Cornwall. Demelza, her name was. The other one worked in the old art gallery. D'you remember the place? Where the hairdresser is now.'

'I remember,' said Sylvia. 'The Something Canvas.'

'*Country* Canvas. They sold all sorts of art supplies, and sometimes had artists at their easels, painting, in the shop window. It was thought to be quite risqué in those days.'

'I remember that,' said Sylvia.

'Think her name was... Fiona? No. Felicity? That was it. Felicity Hope.'

'Oh, Sally's mother,' said Ellie. 'She's now Felicity Jones. So, Sally's mum was Penelope's bridesmaid, and her dad was Felix's best man. That's wild.'

'It's not unusual if you think about it,' Leonard explained. 'It would be like you and Dave being bridesmaid and best man for Sally.'

'Suppose so,' Ellie replied. 'You must have got to know Felix quite well then? What's he like?'

She remembered how, on a previous case, Leonard had contributed very useful information about a young couple in the village who he'd got to know through marrying them.

She didn't mention that they'd spoken to Zane and neither did Sylvia.

'I know he was convicted of fraud, but I always liked Felix. I would never have had him down as a con man. He was funny, charismatic, a brilliant businessman... Was I taken in by him? I don't know. I'd like to think I wasn't.' Leonard paused and Ellie waited to see if he was going to continue. 'People aren't all bad, are they? If you believe in original sin, we're all born with a sinful nature. That means we all have the capacity for sin while retaining the capacity for good also. In my experience, each of us is a mixture of good and bad.' He sighed. 'Alas, I didn't keep in close contact with them after I married them. It's the nature of it unfortunately. You get to know the couple well before the wedding, and afterwards it's just passing in the street, unless they're regular churchgoers.'

'What was their relationship like?' asked Ellie. 'Can you remember?'

It was hard to forget how negatively Zane had spoken about his parents' marriage. And it hadn't been the occasional tiff. He'd said Felix had often threatened to kill Penelope *and* had tried to strangle her.

'From what I remember, they were an attractive couple and very much in love. He adored her. She's always been extremely glamorous. Had quite a few of the men at the tennis club under her spell. That's where they met, you know: at the tennis club. They were both extremely good players and used to partner each other in doubles competitions.'

'In your experience of couples and human nature, would you have Felix down as being capable of killing his wife?'

'Now you're asking. As a man of God, I have to answer that question honestly. Realistically, I suppose I'd have to say about *anyone*: anything is possible if certain circumstances come about. Strong feelings, for example. I do remember he was susceptible to fits of jealousy. But a lot of people are, and they don't murder their partners.'

'And when the news broke of Felix's arrest,' asked Sylvia, 'what did you think? Was it a shock?'

'Yes. Definitely. It's one thing having someone down as a good businessman – but a crook? Someone who carried out art fraud on that sort of scale? I couldn't get my head round it at all. But I married them thirty years ago. Some people stay the same; some change for the better.

Others, life drags them down a route of disappointment or frustration or alienation, and they become criminals...'

Ellie was absorbing what he was saying. She was thinking about Sally – and that they would need to get in touch with her parents – when a scream rang out from the top floor.

Ellie dashed towards the stairs.

There was another scream, even more shrill.

Bridget was on the landing, as pale as a ghost. 'I was having a nap on the bed. Stupidly, I left the door ajar. One of the kittens jumped up with a mouse in its mouth.'

Ellie groaned. 'Oh, goodness.'

'Deposited the thing on my *pillow.*'

'I'm so sorry. That'll be Tallulah.' Ellie peered into the bedroom.

'I'm... I'm terrified of mice.' Bridget grabbed hold of Ellie's arm and tucked herself in behind her body, the way a child might.

On the bed, on the lovely white throw, a tabby kitten was chasing a tiny brown mouse round Bridget's fluffy hot water bottle.

Chapter 13 Day 3 SATURDAY

Ellie was up early the next morning. Before she went to bed, she'd received a call from Zane Wyndham, requesting to meet her at Mistletoe Manor first thing. After learning that Sarge knew both Felix *and* Hargrave, she'd given Sarge a call and asked if he would accompany her. He'd be another pair of ears and eyes, knowledgeable ones too. And given Zoe's new job was tying up her time, Ellie was relieved to have some help.

Ellie walked Rebus and checked the Blix Blitz diary as soon as she'd made a cup of tea. Unless plans changed, she had no cleaning jobs to do herself. Sylvia had agreed to cook breakfast for the B&B guests if she wasn't back in time, so Ellie set the table and put out the condiments, all the while mulling over Penelope's death and wondering what Zane wanted.

Half an hour later, she and Sarge were on the drive at Mistletoe Manor.

'Even bigger than I remember it,' Sarge told her as they approached the house.

They got out and went to join Zane, who was white as snow and trembling.

Ellie introduced Sarge quickly and asked him what the matter was.

'Mum hasn't been paying the rent. The Selbys are furious.' He spoke in snatched sentences. 'They've written to the probate lawyer. We've one week to clear the house of all her property.'

'Oh dear,' said Ellie.

'They're demanding all outstanding rent is paid from her estate.'

Ellie could see Zane was having difficulty absorbing the news. To her, however, it seemed fair enough, if the money was owed.

'Sorry to ask: did your mother have financial problems?' Ellie couldn't help thinking about the brochure Penelope had got from *Yacht World* in the post.

'I... er... don't think so.'

'Then why wouldn't she have paid the rent?'

He shrugged, eyes wide and bewildered.

'Shall we go in?' Ellie deliberately didn't mention that Sarge had grown up with Hargrave. They'd agreed it would be best if Ellie did most of the talking, unless Sarge thought of something important.

The police had handed the crime scene over within twenty-four hours and that meant that Zane was free to do whatever he wanted to at the house.

'Is there any news from your father or Hargrave?' she continued.

'The executor's been in touch,' replied Zane. 'He's in contact with Felix. But nothing from Hargrave.'

Ellie was hoping he'd mention the name of Penelope's beneficiary, but he didn't. 'I'd like to see if we can find anything that will give us a clue as to where the chauffeur is. Shall we look in the bedrooms?'

'I've found some keys,' said Zane. 'Hopefully, one of them will open the room upstairs which was locked when Sylvia was here.'

'Were you and your family planning on coming to the reception here the other night?'

'Yes, although we didn't manage it in the end. The girls were disappointed as they had appointments booked at Santa's grotto at Wootton Castle in the afternoon, and the plan was to come along after those. I know Mum was looking forward to signing and selling lots of books.'

Ellie found herself frowning. It was meant to have been a village event; a post-switching-on-of-the-lights reception, not a book launch. Had there been some sort of a misunderstanding? Had Penelope only offered to host the reception so she could sell books to everyone in the village?

Ellie was trying to figure out how to broach the subject with Zane. She took a deep breath. 'What it seems to suggest was that Penelope was very concerned about how this new book was going to sell and perhaps was struggling for money.' Given what they now knew about the rent, both seemed likely.

She also wanted to ask him why the rental agreement for Mistletoe Manor was in the name of this strange, mystery woman but this, too, seemed a bit sensitive. Perhaps it was best to stay away from conversations about money for a while.

'Shall we go upstairs?'

He nodded. 'I'd like to go into Mum's room. I want to sit amongst her things, spend a bit of time thinking about her...'

A few moments later they were on the landing.

Ellie tried to imagine how Sylvia must have felt, standing here, looking for Penelope when she was downstairs, already dead.

'Sylvia said the room that was locked was the first on the right.' Ellie strode towards the door and tried to turn the handle, but nothing happened. Locked still. She turned to face Zane. 'Have you got the key?'

Zane fished in his pocket and produced a large, circular ring. An assortment of keys hung on this. He tried a few in the lock. The third one opened the door, and they filed in after him.

The room was sparse and bare. Bed, bedside table, wardrobe, chest of drawers. Nothing was on the surfaces. The bed had been used but was made. 'This must've been Hargrave's room,' said Ellie. 'He must have locked it when he left.'

Sarge frowned.

'Don't you think it's odd that Penelope was killed and he left?' Ellie asked. 'Why would anyone do that?'

'Perhaps he left first?' Sarge replied.

'I hadn't thought of that but it's certainly possible,' said Ellie. 'Except – why, in that case, has he not been in touch with the Selbys or Zane, or the police?'

'I have no idea,' said Sarge. 'It's not like him at all.'

Zane frowned. 'Did you know Hargrave, then?' he asked.

Sarge gave Ellie an apologetic look. 'Yes. We grew up together.'

'Oh, good,' said Zane. 'That's going to be useful. No-one seems to know him at all. Where d'you think he's gone?'

Sarge paused and Ellie got the impression he was deciding what to say. 'I don't know. We bumped into each other from time to time, but we weren't in regular contact anymore. I knew he'd taken over from his father as chauffeur here at Mistletoe Manor but that was about it.'

The three of them pottered about in the large bedroom, peering in drawers and opening cupboards.

'He's disappeared into thin air,' Sarge muttered under his breath.

'Yes – why?' asked Ellie.

'I'm just going to pop into Mum's room,' Zane told them. 'Shall I meet you downstairs?'

'Of course. We'll be in the Great Hall.' She wanted to see Penelope's room too but didn't want to infringe on Zane's time in his mum's private space. 'There are a couple of things I'd like to try and figure out down there.'

After a few minutes, Ellie decided they weren't going to find any clues in Hargrave's bedroom, so they filed downstairs to the Great Hall. It was very much as Sylvia had described it. Vast, opulent and dark. Ellie had expected to see the room in disarray, but everything had been tidied and cleaned and polished. They would have a look round.

But Ellie couldn't escape a disconcerting feeling...

Penelope Wyndham had lived and died here... and it was as if she had never been here.

Chapter 14

As soon as they were back from Mistletoe Manor, Ellie and Zoe headed into Deal. It was Saturday, and Zoe's day off.

'I've been here before, with your dad,' Ellie told Zoe, as they approached the record shop in the high street where Toby worked. 'They've changed the name. It used to be called Vince's Vinyls.'

'Dreadful name. Don't blame them for changing it.'

It was an old-fashioned shop, with what looked like the original, wooden windows in a round bay. The panels had been painted white.

The door dinged as it opened, reminding Ellie of the butchers' in the village. Pink Floyd hit their ears, *Dark Side of the Moon,* if she wasn't mistaken.

'You'll have to come back here with Dad. He loves all this old rock music.' Zoe added, 'Hippy music.'

Behind the counter, at the till, a young man was pricing up vinyl, writing on stickers and fixing them on the covers. He wore glasses with thick black rims and a checked, peaked cap.

'That's him,' Zoe whispered. 'I recognise him from photos in the local paper.'

'Hi there,' he said, looking up from what he was doing. 'Are you just browsing today, or can I help you with anything?'

'We're actually here to see you,' Ellie told him. She introduced Zoe and herself. 'We're private investigators, looking into the murder of Penelope Wyndham.'

Briefly, he froze. 'Oh right.'

'We're here because we know about the legal dispute between the two of you.'

Ellie was studying him carefully and a profound blush swept over his cheeks and neck.

'Can I ask when you last saw her?'

'I spoke to the police yesterday. I don't have anything further to add.'

Ellie had encountered this sort of response before. Some people were happy to talk to them, others were not. It was understandable.

'That's fine. We don't work with the police though.' She didn't say they were helping the family as it might not endear them to him. 'Would you mind repeating what you told them?'

He didn't answer.

Ellie glanced at Zoe, using her eyes to convey a request for help. The young man looked about five years older than Zoe. Perhaps she'd have more luck with him.

'I'll be over here,' Ellie told Zoe, 'looking for a present for your dad.'

'Are you the Pink Floyd fan?' Zoe asked gently.

'No, I am *not*,' he replied emphatically. 'I cannot stand them. If I have to listen to any more of David Gilmour's whiny guitar and nasal vocals, I'm going to run down the street screaming.' He rolled his eyes, as if he hadn't already made his point. 'The shop owner leaves a playlist of albums. Unfortunately, some of the others are even worse. Led Zeppelin, Whitesnake. Ugh.'

'Golly. I know exactly how you feel. My dad is obsessed with David Gilmour. Can't play a note on the guitar yet every time the solos come on...' she dropped her voice, pretending she didn't want her mum to hear, 'he's up on the sofa strumming away at whatever object he can get hold of. Last time I think it was a lamp.'

Toby chuckled conspiratorially.

'Oh, my goodness, embarrassing or what?' Zoe continued. 'And he thinks he looks cool.'

'The shop owner is exactly the same. He even does that ecstasy-agony face the oldies pull when they're pretending to hold a vibrating note on a guitar solo. Mega cringe.'

Ellie was finding it hard not to laugh. Zoe was enjoying herself a bit too much.

While the two twenty-somethings continued their conversation, Ellie looked round the shop. It really was the vinyl lover's paradise. Rows of racks around the circumference of the room, stuffed full of vinyl albums, singles, 12-inches.

'What do you listen to?' Zoe asked. 'I'm really into Bastille, Glass Animals and Twenty One Pilots at the moment.'

Ellie was pleased Zoe was here to talk music with Toby.

'Bastille are really cool,' he replied. 'Saw them at Latitude last year.'

Then she heard Zoe ask, 'Are you managing to fit a bit of writing round working here?'

Ellie kept her head down, pretending she couldn't hear. Pretending to look at the records, lifting them out one at a time, studying the front or the back of the sleeve and frowning knowledgeably. She was going to have to buy one.

'A bit. Although I've lost a lot of enthusiasm.' Toby scrunched his nose and his voice changed. 'It all feels pointless.'

Zoe gave him a kind smile. 'It's difficult when stuff happens, isn't it? It affects your confidence and makes you wonder whether it's worth carrying on.'

He nodded.

'For a long time I wanted to work in wildlife photography, but it's so difficult to get into. Lots of nepotism and mutual back-scratching.'

'What do you do now, then?' asked Toby. 'I notice you used the past tense there.'

'I haven't given up photography completely. I work for a wildlife rescue charity and love it. I do a lot of their photography so I'm still getting practice. It's just not as exciting as spending hours on the cliffs trying to get shots of hunting birds or in fields, catching hares on the run.'

'The shop owner is always teasing me,' said Toby. 'I write the recommendation cards.' He pointed at a piece of white card which had handwriting on it, telling buyers what to expect from that album and artist. 'Keeps saying, "You should be a writer..."'

'You could have a bash at music journalism. You sound knowledgeable.'

He shrugged.

'Does your boss know what happened with Mrs Wyndham? It sounds awful. So traumatic, when you pay money and trust someone to help you...'

'Yep. He does.' Sadness washed over him.

'Courses are expensive, aren't they?' said Zoe. 'I won a competition six months ago. The prize was amazing – one of Chris Packham's photography courses. Luckily, that helped me a lot and it only cost me the entrance fee.'

'Yeah, I spent all my savings on that flipping course with Penelope. I did learn stuff but...' he shrugged sadly, 'the rest is history.'

'Were you at least able to get your money back?'

He shook his head. 'I had to drop the case.'

Ellie's ears pricked up and she almost squealed with excitement. She held her breath, hoping he was going to reveal what happened.

'That's such a shame. Why?' Zoe whispered.

'Someone didn't want me to continue with it...'

'You mean Penelope?'

'Oh, I'm sure she didn't but, no, I don't mean her. Although whether she initiated it, I've no idea. But... someone paid me a visit in a *dark alley*.' He emphasised the words, as though they were self-explanatory. 'Must have been following me. Threatened to kill me unless I dropped the legal action.'

Zoe gasped.

Ellie was having to strain her ears to hear over the top of Pink Floyd.

'That's awful,' said Zoe. 'You must have been terrified. Did you tell the police?'

'Do you mean at the time or this morning?'

'Well, both.'

'Oh yes. Unfortunately, there was no CCTV in the alley. Presumably, that's why they chose that place to jump me.' He put his hand on his chest. 'I really struggle to go out in the dark now. Can just about manage a busy main road with lights... but dark lanes...' His voice broke. 'And alleys...' He shuddered.

Ellie felt a surge of sympathy. This was terrible. If what Toby was saying was true, he'd had his work stolen by someone he trusted. Then had been scared into dropping his legal case for reparation and been left with what sounded like PTSD or a sort of agoraphobia. Was it safe, then, to assume Toby wouldn't have been tramping across the lanes and fields to Mistletoe Manor to murder Penelope? They'd need to wait until they'd heard both sides before deciding.

Zoe carried on talking. 'Did you see who it was in the alley? Or get any clues?'

He shook his head. 'They were wearing black clothes and a balaclava.'

'Male or female?'

'Pretty sure it was a male. Lanky. Grunted as he went for me.'

'And the police weren't able to find them on the CCTV leading to the alley? Catch whoever it was on the way there or back?'

'Unfortunately not.'

'That's such bad luck. What did your lawyer say? And the police? Did they think the threat was real?'

'Oh yes. It wasn't a death threat from a keyboard warrior. The person took the time to deliver the threat in person. To risk getting caught. And made sure it was delivered with enough menace to scare me.'

'What d'you mean?'

'Let's just say that they told me how they'd end my life and demonstrated...' He looked Zoe in the eye. 'They put a cord round my neck.'

Chapter 15

Sylvia tied the last bow just as *Away in a Manger* was finishing. She applied a smattering of red glitter glue to the wrapping paper and placed the parcel with the others, under the tree in the lounge.

Ellie had just got back from the record shop and had nipped upstairs for a shower. While the madeleines were in the oven, Sylvia had taken the opportunity to wrap Ellie's present – new Ugg boots she'd been hankering after for the last month, to replace the ones that Reeby had chewed.

'You didn't mean to, did you, boy?'

Rebus tilted his head, listening.

'You got confused. Thought they were your toys, didn't you?' She stroked his ears. 'You and Tallulah aren't in your mum's good books,' she told him, chuckling about the kitten's antics. The mouse had been caught and deposited safely outside, and Bridget said she'd keep their room door shut from now on.

Sylvia was mulling over the photo she'd taken of Penelope's notepad. She brought the image up on her phone. The top of the 'L' tailed off, presumably the last part of the letter she'd written. Perhaps, because the woman had been writing it in a rush, she'd had the notepad at an angle? Sylvia rotated it one hundred and eighty degrees and it became the number '7'. Hmm. What could that mean?

Seven people?

Seven o'clock?

She had no idea. It might not mean anything.

She packed away the paper, ribbon, glitter, Sellotape and scissors and went to check on the oven, singing along to the descant in *Hark! The Herald* at the top of her voice.

Once the madeleines were out, she placed the baking tray on the worktop and pressed the sponge lightly with her finger to check the resistance. Perfect. Firm with a little give. They were Leonard's favourite, particularly when she dipped them in Belgian chocolate.

The warm, buttery, vanilla aroma made her mouth water.

She turned to the full-length mirror on the kitchen wall and checked her side profile admiringly. She and Ellie had been on a diet for the last two months. Lost half a stone each in preparation for Christmas.

There was a rap at the door.

Rebus shot across the kitchen, squealing like he was about to die if he didn't get to whoever was there. Sylvia smiled. This noise of his differentiated people he knew from those he didn't – but Rebus adored everyone, so it wasn't much of a clue. It was either he didn't know the visitor or adored them.

Car doors slammed. Voices.

She opened up and DS Carmichael was facing her.

'Oh–'

The detective wasn't alone. Dave stood next to her, a regretful expression on both their faces. Behind them, several paces back, were two uniformed officers.

Sylvia saw him swallow. 'I'm really sorry, Mum.' He stepped aside, giving his sergeant a nod.

Rebus sidled up to Sylvia, tail between his legs, and sat by her side, glancing at Dave reproachfully.

She gasped as DS Carmichael said the phrase she'd heard so many times on TV.

'Sylvia Valerie Blix, I'm arresting you on suspicion of the murder of Penelope Wyndham.'

'What? No.'

'You do not have to say anything.'

'There must be some mistake. Why on earth would I want to kill Penelope?'

'But it may harm your defence if you do not mention when questioned something which you later rely on in court.'

A wave of dizziness swept over Sylvia. It was as if the room was spinning.

'Anything you do say may be given in evidence. Do you understand?'

Sylvia nodded.

'What's going on?' Ellie shouted down, concern echoing in her voice.

Dave spoke now. 'Ells, can you come down?'

'Hang on, I've just got out of the shower.'

There was shuffling on the stairs and Ellie appeared, wet hair and a bath towel wrapped round her.

'What's going on?' She looked at Sylvia, taking in the scene.

'We've arrested your mother-in-law on suspicion of Penelope Wyndham's murder,' DS Carmichael replied.

'On what basis?'

'I'm afraid we're unable to tell you anything more than that at the present moment,' said the sergeant. 'Do you want us to call you when she's free to go home?'

'Please,' whispered Ellie.

'If you could come with us, please, Mrs Blix?' said DS Carmichael. 'We'll be taking you to the police station.'

'Hang on. Can we drop her off some food?'

But they'd gone before Ellie got an answer.

Chapter 16

Ellie stood in the doorway, heart hammering in her chest, watching the police cars leave with Sylvia, red tail-lights disappearing down the drive and onto Pennypot Lane. She clung to the door, trying to absorb what had just happened.

Rebus whined.

'It's OK, boy. We'll have her home soon.'

DS Carmichael's words rang in her mind.

'... arresting you on suspicion of the murder of Penelope Wyndham.'

This was serious. For the police to arrest Sylvia, they must have evidence.

Ellie was about to go in, when, with a gulp of dread, she spotted her B&B guests walking up the drive, sheepish expressions on their faces.

She couldn't help groaning. It was bad enough that their stay had begun the day of Penelope's death. First, one of their hosts had found the body. Then there'd been the mouse incident. Now the same host had been arrested for murder... and the other was standing on the doorstep in a towel.

'Was that Sylvia the police have just... er...?' asked Bridget, eyes wide with alarm.

Ellie cringed.

'... nicked?' Nigel finished his wife's sentence, face flushed with excitement, seemingly less alarmed than his wife and less concerned about being nosey.

Bridget clapped her hand over her mouth. 'Oh, Nigel.' She clung to his arm. 'This is terrifying. I thought villages were safe.'

Ellie felt like sloping inside and hiding but knew she couldn't. 'Please don't worry. There's been a misunderstanding. I'm sure it'll be resolved quickly.' Should she leave it there, or refer back to what Zoe had told Bridget about Sylvia's husband putting Felix Wyndham in prison? Say it was likely to be some kind of set-up for revenge? 'I'm so sorry this has coincided with your stay,' she said instead in a tired voice. 'I'm a bit embarrassed. Lower Wootton is usually such a quiet place.'

Nigel spoke now. 'Everyone's talking about it in the shops. We've just had coffee at the Rattling Cat at the other end of the village.' He sucked in air dramatically. 'You should hear the gossip down there. Someone was saying the victim's husband did it and–'

'Do you need me for anything or...?' asked Ellie sweetly, keen to get away from their questions. At this rate, Bridget was going to be hotfooting it back to London.

'Oh, no. Thank you.' Bridget blushed. 'We've just popped back to get an extra layer of clothes.'

Ellie politely asked them about their plans for the evening and made her excuses as quickly as she could. If she was going to continue with B&B guests, she was going to have to get better at handling boundaries. She was desperate to think about Sylvia, to rack her brain for ideas. What could possibly have happened for the police to decide they needed to arrest her?

Ellie went back inside and closed the door. She shuffled into the lounge and settled cross-legged on the sofa where the kittens were sleeping. She knew enough from Dave to be sure they would not have arrested Sylvia unless they were certain it was necessary, particularly since she was Dave's mum. Not that they weren't careful with other people, just that they were likely to be doubly careful, knowing how upsetting it would be for Dave and the family.

She needed to ring Zoe. Sylvia was her grandmother and Zoe would want to know what was going on. She slid her phone out of her pocket and dialled.

'Hey Mum.'

'Where are you?'

'Just parked near Hambrook Marshes. I'm collecting a swan that's hurt its wing. What's up?'

'I'm afraid I've got bad news. Are we on loudspeaker?'

'It's OK. It's just me here.'

She told Zoe about Sylvia's arrest.

Zoe gasped. 'For Penelope's murder?' Her voice broke. 'Why do they think she did it?'

As Ellie explained that the police weren't able to give any information, Zoe began sniffing.

'That's crazy though.' Zoe started to cry. 'We've got to help her.' She blew her nose. 'I hope they don't put her in a room without a window like on TV. She gets claustrophobic.'

'Oh, sweetie. Don't worry. We'll get her out.' Ellie waited for a few moments. 'Your dad and the team will be doing everything they can to establish the facts, I'm sure.'

Zoe sniffed again.

Ellie continued. 'Whatever has come up suggesting she's guilty, they'll be picking it over with a fine-tooth comb.'

'I can't get out of my head that Penelope wanted Gran to do her catering,' Zoe replied. 'It's hard not to wonder if it was a setup.'

'I know what you mean. It is odd. But who knows? Maybe she didn't bear any ill-feeling towards Sylvia. Simply accepted that your granddad was doing his job, and it was nothing to do with his wife. Genuinely wanted Sylvia to do the canapés for the party.'

'The thing is, because Gran found Penelope's body, she was on the spot. Think about it. She'd be the perfect person for someone to set up as the murderer if they wanted to deflect attention away from themselves.'

'Hmm,' said Ellie. 'It's not good, is it? I've been wondering if that's a possibility too. Alternatively, perhaps they found some forensic information at the crime scene which, at face value, incriminates Sylvia?'

'It's possible. Maybe she leaned over the body to see if Penelope was dead, and the crime scene staff have picked up her DNA or some transfer evidence.'

'That's what it'll be.' Ellie wanted to reassure Zoe – and herself. 'Something innocent. They know Sylvia was there. She told them. She'll be released in no time, I'm sure.'

But Ellie sensed, in the pit of her stomach, there was more to it. Would Sylvia have been arrested for something like that?

Zoe wasn't convinced either. 'Crime scene evidence can take ages to analyse. The labs are inundated. I don't like the idea of poor Gran having to stay in a cell overnight.'

'I don't either. I'm sure it won't come to that.'

'I wonder why they didn't just ask her to attend the police station for an interview under caution?'

They were both silent for a few moments.

'I'm going to text Dad. See if he knows how long she might be. If he can't tell me, or doesn't know, he can just say so.'

'OK, lovey.'

'I need to get off my phone to do that. I'll call you straight back, OK?' Zoe rang off.

Rebus jumped up onto the sofa next to Ellie, snuggling in beside her and dispensing a quick lick on her cheek.

Her thoughts continued to churn. What if the killer had still been in the room where Penelope was killed when Sylvia got there? What if he or she had seen Sylvia arrive and decided to frame her? If they knew the property, they could easily have made their exit while Sylvia was calling 999 and waiting for the police.

Zoe came back through. 'Dad won't say how long she'll be or what grounds they've got for arresting her.'

'Oh well. We tried. It was unlikely he was going to tell us.'

'But – Gran asked him to give us a message. It was: "*What did Penelope say to Zoe just after she switched on the lights?*"'

'What *did* she say to you?' asked Ellie.

'That she was in a hurry to get back to Mistletoe Manor because someone was following her.'

Ellie gasped.

'That's why she was late,' said Zoe. 'They'd taken a detour. Everything's been so manic, and there was so much noise at the lights, I'd forgotten completely. I think I dismissed it as a joke, or as her being deliberately dramatic so she could make an entrance.'

'Wow. That's very definite. She didn't say she *thought* someone was following her?'

'Nope. Someone *was* following her. And, before you ask, no, she didn't say who. However – now I think back, she was a bit jumpy. She kept looking over her shoulder and scanning the crowd.'

Ellie was absorbing the news.

'We need an emergency team meeting,' said Zoe. 'I've got half an hour free at lunchtime today. Let's meet at the pub at 12.30pm. We're a woman down. Finn and Charlie and the band are playing a gig in there this evening, so I'll see if Finn can join us for a bit while they're setting up.'

'Good idea. I'll bring Sarge. I haven't got round to telling you this yet, but he knows Felix and Hargrave.'

Chapter 17

Hawksdown, the disused WWI airfield, looked beautiful in the snow. The miles of open fields were one of Ellie's favourite walking spots in all seasons. She strode purposefully, arms swinging, her eyes low. The falling snow was returning the grey slush on the plateau of chalk grassland to a white blanket.

As she walked, deep in thought, cold flakes landed on her cheeks. Her thoughts ran to Sylvia in custody. Hopefully, they'd brought her a cup of tea and she wasn't too scared; and was coping with having to wait in a small room.

She tried to piece together the shocking awfulness of Penelope's death, and all the things they'd learned about her life and the people around her. Everyone, it seemed, had deserted her apart from her beloved son. Felix was in hiding somewhere. Hargrave, the loyal chauffeur, had done a runner and Penelope had not just alienated the young writer, Toby. She had, if his account was to be believed, stolen his work and someone had made it their business to prevent him from pursuing legal action.

There was something about Toby that bothered Ellie, but she couldn't quite put her finger on it; something to do with his manner. She would mull it over further as she walked, see if she could pinpoint it.

Thank goodness for these wonderful fields. She'd walked in them all her life: as a child with her parents; at school; as a young adult, and with Dave for decades. She found the open expanse freeing, comforting, containing. The rhythmic movement of walking seemed to shake her thoughts free, to encourage lurking ideas to make themselves known.

In the distance, she saw a figure striding towards her, waving their arms frantically. She recognised the lolloping movements of Luna, Sally's dog.

'Who's that, Reeby?'

He pricked up his ears, turned in Luna's direction and made a dash towards her. The two dogs started leaping about in the snow, a picture of innocence and fun.

Ellie waved back. Sally must want something. Hopefully it wasn't an emergency.

'I've been phoning you,' said Sally, when she got within earshot.

'Oh, sorry. I've got such thick clothes on, my phone's in my pocket. I didn't hear it ring. What's up?'

'Mum's been on the phone,' said Sally.

The two women started walking.

'Katie Douglas has been round, asking Mum questions about Penelope Wyndham.'

Katie was a journalist on the local newspaper, renowned for her lack of ethical reporting.

'I was wondering when she was going to start looking into Felix's past and doing her usual stirring,' Ellie told her friend.

'I had no idea Mum and Dad knew Penelope and Felix,' said Sally.

'Leonard told us yesterday. He officiated at their wedding.'

'From what I've gathered,' Sally continued, 'Felix and Penelope were a bit older than Mum and Dad. They all became friends at the tennis club. It was very couple-y and they used to play doubles together.'

'What was Katie asking your mum, then?'

'All sorts. She's obviously been digging up the dirt. Poor Mum. She was really upset. Bad enough an old friend being murdered. Then to have Katie stirring everything up with her questions. I'm absolutely furious. Dad was out. He'd gone to the butcher's to collect their meat order for Christmas. So, Mum had to contend with Katie on her own. You know what that woman's like...'

'Yeah. A dog with a bone – on amphetamines.'

Ellie – and many others – had had run-ins with Katie over the hatchet-job pieces she wrote about people in the village.

Ellie retrieved her phone from her pocket. There were three missed call notifications from Sally on her screen. She unmuted Google alerts for Katie Douglas and the *Wootton Gazette*.

'I wonder why she didn't want to speak to your dad too?'

'She did. It's just that Dad was out. I haven't spoken to him yet. Katie may well have tracked him down in the village or at the butcher's. I'll find out once he's back. That woman's got the brass neck of a trombone.'

As they walked, Ellie was thinking. The four of them must've been close for Sally's parents to have had official roles at their wedding.

'Mum told me she's got something to tell you. Something she didn't tell Katie at the newspaper.'

Ellie stopped walking. 'What?'

'She didn't say. She's going out shortly and said can you come round this evening at 6pm?'

Chapter 18

When Ellie and Sarge arrived, the Windmill Inn was packed. Under the low beams of the sixteenth-century pub, carols tinkled over the music system. A large tree stood in one of the bay windows, a mass of tinsel, baubles and glittering fairy lights. If it weren't for Penelope's death, everything might've looked normal for the week before Christmas: mainly locals and a few out-of-towners.

The band were doing a soundcheck on the stage in the corner. Charlie waved.

Zoe and Finn were already there, sitting at a large table by one of the open fires. Rebus was stretched out on the warm hearth, basking in the heat, the loop of his lead round Zoe's chair leg.

The new pub management had recently changed to doing food all day, and staff scuttled about, carrying plates from and to the kitchen. Delicious smells wafted around the bar. Sausages and mash. Shepherd's pie. Battered cod. Lasagne.

Finn was tucking into a toasted sandwich with chips.

Zoe had a sandwich too, which she'd barely touched. Her eyes were red, and a packet of tissues sat beside her plate. 'I've rung the police station again.' Her voice was wobbly. 'Still no news on Gran. I asked if we could see her, and they said no.'

'I'll get drinks,' Sarge told Ellie softly. 'What would you like?'

'A Diet Coke, please.'

Ellie caught Finn's raised eyebrow as Sarge walked away.

'He's looking sprightly these days,' Finn said quietly. 'I'd hardly have thought he was the same man.' He pulled a chair out for Ellie.

Ellie explained about the cortisone injection.

Zoe pushed her plate towards her mum. 'We've got to get Gran home.' She wiped her nose on a tissue. 'Finn and I have made a list of questions.'

Ellie sat down.

'Most importantly,' Zoe continued, 'we need to know what the evidence is that's led to the arrest.'

'Presumably the police will discuss it with Sylvia,' Ellie replied. 'They aren't going to tell us. But – we *can* discuss the options.'

'We've started on that already,' Zoe replied, her cheeks flushing with intensity. 'It's got to be more than her fingerprints being at the crime scene. Her DNA, even.'

'Exactly,' said Ellie. 'And she found the body but didn't touch it so there should be nothing from Sylvia on Penelope.'

'Finn and I reckon it's got to be decisive evidence otherwise they'd simply interview her under caution.'

'Yes,' said Finn as he wiped his fingers on his napkin. 'What would the most compelling evidence be?'

Ellie didn't need to think about that. 'CCTV showing her carrying out the act. Except that's not possible because she didn't do it.'

'Ah.' Finn pointed with his finger. 'What if someone's faked exactly that? I saw a video on the internet yesterday which looked completely real but had been created with AI. You'd just need someone good with technology.'

'That's rather scary,' Ellie said. 'I suppose we can't rule it out.'

Sarge arrived back with their drinks. He passed Ellie her glass of Coke and sat down with his pint of real ale from the local Hawkshill Brewery. 'Cleaned up that mess you left the outhouse in, so I did,' he said, staring at Zoe.

'Sorree. I was going to do it after work, honestly. You beat me to it. Thank you.' Zoe smiled at the man who was old enough to be her great-grandfather. He'd become like family to them all.

Ellie filled him in on what they'd been discussing.

'How do you know Hargrave then?' Zoe asked Sarge.

He told them about the youth club. Living close when they were growing up. His real name.

'Greg Wood sounds very different from "Hargrave", doesn't it?' Finn glanced at Zoe.

'Hargrave sounds much more like a country house chauffeur,' replied Zoe.

'Another thing that'll help Sylvia is us gathering information on the other key suspects,' said Ellie. 'If we can prove someone else did it, that gets Sylvia off the hook.'

'I agree,' said Zoe.

Ellie continued. 'Zane told us yesterday that his father had tried to strangle Penelope before. Also using fairy lights. And was regularly threatening to kill her. That's got to make Felix our number one suspect, surely?' She glanced round.

'I'd say so,' said Sarge.

'Felix, suspect number one,' Ellie counted on her fingers. 'Let's double down on finding him. Agreed?'

Everyone nodded.

'Suspect number two, we have Toby Drysdale,' she continued. 'He has a motive. And number three... you're not going to like this, Sarge, we've got to include Hargrave at this point. His disappearance does not suggest innocence.'

Sarge sighed. 'What possible motive could he have though?' he asked sadly.

Ellie shrugged. 'Until we – or the police – find him, we won't know.'

'They can't think he's guilty or they wouldn't have arrested Sylvia,' Sarge replied. 'Not that I'm suggesting *she* is, of course.'

'Except that if they haven't found him yet,' said Zoe, 'they might not have been able to establish where he was when she was killed. That means they might not have discounted or included him.'

Sarge cleared his throat. 'I'll stick my neck out here. I'm certain something must've happened for him to disappear.'

'He's your friend though,' Ellie told him. 'It's bound to make you biased.'

'True, and Sylvia's *your* mother-in-law but I don't say *you're* biased, thinking she's innocent.' Sarge's response was understandably prickly. 'I'll go round to his parents' house. See if they still live there and have heard from him.'

'Let's not argue,' said Zoe promptly. 'Perhaps Hargrave was worried he'd come under suspicion?' She paused. 'Anyway, let's move on for now. I've been doing a bit more digging into the Wyndham family. Specifically, the son.'

'What've you found?'

'Zane is launching a new energy drink under his Wyndham Wellness brand. Caffeine-free, made of all natural ingredients...'

'Yawn,' muttered Sarge.

'Launching in January, it's called ShilaPeak and is made from shilajit minerals, lion's mane mushrooms and seamoss.'

'Ugh,' said Ellie. 'I definitely won't be trying it. I don't like mushrooms at the best of times, but these weird-sounding ones freak me out.'

Zoe continued. 'These ingredients are meant to have amazing properties. This is me talking here now. They're thought to combat fatigue, support brain health and reduce inflammation.'

'That'll be one for you and your gran then,' Ellie told her. 'Along with the Wim Hof flipping breathing you've got her doing. If I have to listen to that man's voice once more, I'm going to...'

'Oh, I'm so pleased she's doing it,' said Zoe, beaming at her mum. 'It activates the parasympathetic branch of the–'

'Enough, enough,' said Ellie. 'I can't take all this woo nonsense. Going back to Zane's new drink – what's this got to do with Penelope?'

'This is the other interesting bit. Zane developed it when he was in the US looking after his mother. She took shilajit for its neuroprotective properties and lion's mane for its anti-inflammatory ones, and she credits them for her recovery from meningitis.'

'Oh, wow,' said Ellie. 'That makes me feel I should be a bit less dismissive.'

Zoe nodded. 'It also shows how committed Zane is to his mother.'

Chapter 19

Ellie was in the garden at the windmill, shovelling the snow from the path and patio. She'd stopped to watch the kittens. This cold snap was the first time they'd seen snow. Tally, who was still smaller than her sister, was tip-toeing over the frozen ground, flicking her paws, and Cleo was trying to catch individual snowflakes in her mouth, only to find they dissolved. The cream patch under Cleo's chin caught the light each time she moved.

The kitchen window opened outwards. Finn's voice boomed from inside. 'Ellie? Phone.' He waved the landline receiver in the air. 'It's urgent.' He had dropped round to collect a spare set of clothes for Zoe, who'd got her jeans wet, trying to rescue an injured mallard after lunch.

Ellie scuttled inside.

'It's Caroline from Blix Blitz.' Finn scrunched his nose up, presumably hoping to warn Ellie about something unpleasant.

Her heart sank. She took the phone and put it to her ear.

'... is doing my nut,' came Caroline's strident voice. 'I've had enough. So far, she's told me I'm not vacuuming right, I shouldn't clean the mirrors with the vinegar spray we've always used, and I've got to move every single piece of furniture while she watches me. *Every single flippin' piece.* Why does she need to watch me?'

'OK. Calm dow–'

'I'm not doing it, Ellie. I'm sorry but it's too much. I've already hurt my shoulder trying to lift her massive bed. The frame must be made of concrete.'

'I take it this is Mrs Andrews?'

'Yeah. Who else? She's always been a nightmare, but this is next level. Honestly, she's got worse and worse. She never used to be here when we cleaned. Now she refuses to leave. Has she all of a sudden decided she doesn't trust us?'

'OK. Pack up your stuff and tell her I'll be there in fifteen minutes. I'll do her clean. Don't have a row with her. Just leave quietly and politely. I'm leaving now.'

Fifteen minutes later, Ellie was in Mrs Andrews' lounge. On the way over, she'd had a think about what she wanted to say.

'I'm not paying for her to spend the whole time chatting to her mum about who's having what for dinner,' Mrs Andrews told Ellie, 'and whether they're going to have goose or turkey on Christmas Day.' She stood, hands on hips by the fireplace, adjusting the position of some candles on the mantelpiece.

Ellie frowned. 'What d'you mean, she's chatting to her mum?'

'Got her phone on speaker, hasn't she?'

'But she's cleaning too?'

The woman shrugged. 'If you can call it that. She keeps missing bits.'

'Is it the speaker you're not keen on or how she's cleaning?'

'Both.'

'But you *were* happy with it, weren't you? I've checked the records, and you haven't made any complaints or raised any concerns.'

'No.'

'Has something changed then? Is the speaker thing new?'

'Yes. But it's not just that.' Tears welled up in Mrs Andrews' eyes.

Ellie paused while the older woman fetched a tissue from the coffee table.

'I'll happily ask Caroline not to conduct personal conversations while she's doing your cleaning.'

A tear rolled down the woman's cheek and she blew her nose.

'Would that solve things for you? Or...' Ellie softened her voice. 'Or is there something else?'

'It's my mum.'

Ellie waited.

'She passed away a few weeks ago and–' A sob burst from her.

'I'm so sorry.'

Mrs Andrews grabbed another tissue from the box. She dabbed at her face and composed herself. 'I'd love to chat to my mum about plans for Christmas–'

'... of course.'

'... but I'm never going to speak to her again.' Her voice broke. 'It's too... too painful to listen to Caroline–' She stopped there.

'I understand. And Caroline will too.' Ellie collected her thoughts. 'Do you want us to move every item of furniture when we clean? If so, I'll need to send two peop–'

Mrs Andrews shook her head. 'It's fine, if she's not on her phone and is concentrating.'

'No problem.' Ellie checked again that the woman was happy with this and changed the subject. 'Have you got plans for Christmas?'

Mrs Andrews nodded. 'My sister and her husband are coming here.' She gestured to the tree in the bay window. A warm light reflected off gold tinsel and red baubles. 'Got that from the farm shop. There's a new chap selling them and doing logs. I'm usually dreadful with names but couldn't forget this one. Felix. Same as this fella.' She gestured to the ginger cat, who was curled up on an armchair, purring loudly. 'Felix Wyndham.'

Chapter 20

At the police station, once Dave's team had carried out the custody formalities with Sylvia, she was taken to an interview room where DS Carmichael and another detective were waiting for her on one side of a table and chairs. Adamant she was innocent, Sylvia had refused legal advice.

DS Carmichael ushered her to a seat opposite them and waited until she was settled. 'I'll be conducting your interviews as you and DI Blix are related.'

The last time Sylvia had been in an interview room had been with a social work client, and it had been very different being *with* the person who was accused rather than *being* them.

And this room was much smaller.

But she knew she hadn't killed Penelope, so she'd have to trust the process and hope they would figure out who the murderer was and let her go home.

As the sergeant spoke, many of the questions seemed to repeat what Dave had asked her when he'd come to the windmill. What time had she got to Mistletoe Manor? What had she gone there for? Why was she doing Penelope's catering?

She repeated the answers she'd given Dave, aware they were doing their job, double-checking, dotting 'i's and crossing 't's. She knew enough about police work to realise there had to be more to what they thought they knew than this.

And then came the information she'd been waiting for...

'We have a witness who saw you strangle Penelope Wyndham,' DS Carmichael told her in a low voice. 'What do you say to that?'

Thoughts were firing through Sylvia's mind. 'They're lying. Penelope was dead when I got to the Great Hall. I've told you.'

'The witness says they saw you enter the hall, get into an argument with Mrs Wyndham, yank a section of fairy lights off the tree and strangle her.'

'Who is this witness?'

'We cannot share that information.'

'How can I assess the truth of what you're claiming if I don't know the source?'

'That's for us to establish, Mrs Blix. All you need to do is answer the questions.'

Sylvia tutted impatiently. She knew the police had to have verified their witness' account. 'OK, if you can't tell me who they are, where are they claiming they saw me do this from? There was nobody at Mistletoe Manor when I arrived, unless they were hiding.'

DS Carmichael glanced sideways at her colleague.

'All I can do is repeat what you know already,' said Sylvia. 'I was at the house. Penelope was expecting me and was dead when I arrived.' She paused as a thought popped into her mind. 'However – it occurs to me that someone might have been there, and I didn't see them. But whoever it was most certainly did *not* see me strangle Penelope.'

The male detective checked his notes.

'And if someone was there, it would make me wonder what they were doing – and whether in fact *they* strangled Penelope.'

Chapter 21

Lower Wootton farm shop was on the main road out of the village. When Ellie arrived, it was a hive of activity. People were getting in and out of vehicles, loading string bags of logs into their car boots and strapping Christmas trees to their roof racks. The door to the shop was open and *Away in a Manger* was blasting out.

Ellie checked her phone for news about Sylvia but there was nothing. She surveyed the scene for signs of someone taking money for the trees, but she couldn't see anyone. She walked into the shop and headed straight for the cash desk, where a stressed-looking woman, wearing reindeer horns, was changing a till roll while a line of customers waited impatiently.

'Hi. Have you got someone called Felix working here? One of the locals said she bought a Christmas tree from him?'

'Yeah. You should find him in one of the barns at the back. Do you want to go out and speak to him or would you like to leave a message? Lots of customers are leaving their numbers. He's doing log deliveries as well, if you're interested.'

'Thanks. I'll just pop out and have a word with him. It's probably easier. Where am I looking when I get out there?'

She gave Ellie instructions.

A couple of minutes later Ellie was heading towards a large barn. As she approached, a rhythmical thudding sound hit her ears: an axe going into wood.

She knew what Felix looked like. They'd seen photos of him during the police investigation into his fraud, but they were all from before he went to prison. In those days, his look was very much that of the country gent: corduroy trousers, tweed jackets, tan-coloured brogues.

Peering round the entrance, she saw a short, silver-haired man. He had a tool belt around his waist over workmen's trousers and various layers of jumpers. His slice of the axe was decisive and strong, despite his slight build. The court records had him down as sixty-three years old.

A radio was playing Slade's *Merry Xmas Everybody*. On one wall, a wood-burning stove was belching out heat, copper flames dancing inside the grate. To the left of where he was standing was a large pile of wood. To the right was a pile of neatly chopped sections in different sizes.

'Felix? I'm Ellie Blix from Lower Wootton.'

He looked up, holding a raised axe in the air for a few moments before he whacked it through the log beneath his foot. Was he trying to intimidate her?

'We've been looking for you for a few days.'

'Here I am.' He raised his axe and brought it down again, splitting another log. 'Heard you and your family were poking about.'

Ellie was curious about who he'd been talking to, but quickly realised it didn't really matter. People were inevitably talking in the village, what with Penelope's death coming after her husband's release.

Usually, she asked people's permission before she started firing questions at them, but instinct told her to plunge in. The police would already have paid Felix a visit and asked him where he was when Penelope was killed. Although this was what she wanted to know, she was aware that it might cause his defences to spring up and the conversation would be over.

'Didn't see you at the switching-on of the lights the other day...'

'That's because I wasn't there. Working, wasn't I? Thursdays are my Ripple delivery days. Great Mongeham too, if I can fit it in.'

'Your customers will vouch for you, will they?'

'Certain of it.'

Deciding it was best not to mention his art galleries, she replied, 'One of my cleaning clients told me about your Christmas trees. You dropped her off a beauty.'

'And before you ask: yes, they are legit. Got every man and his dog watching me now, haven't I?'

'Where are you living?'

He looked up, for the first time stopping his chopping. 'At the Rattling Cat. I'm helping with their deliveries, the cellar, picking up glasses, all the jobs no one else wants to do. But they give me bed and board and all my meals, so I shouldn't complain.'

'I would have thought you'd stay at Beech Farm?'

He snorted. 'That would have been handy, although I'd still have needed to earn a living.'

Ellie wanted to know why Felix hadn't gone back into the art world. However, this also might make him clam up. She was racking her brain for how she could ask about it without being too direct.

'Got my parole officer breathing down my neck as well. Thanks to my *wife*.' He emphasised the word angrily.

Ellie immediately thought of what Zane had told them about Felix attempting to strangle Penelope, and threatening to kill her numerous times.

'It must be very difficult, making a fresh start,' said Ellie. 'It's not a coincidence that I'm here. I'd prefer to be honest with you.'

'I didn't think you'd come to buy a Christmas tree.'

'We are investigating your wife's *murder*.'

She used the word deliberately, instead of death, so as to be able to assess his response.

'My son got you doing that?'

'No. My mother-in-law wanted to investigate.'

'Did she now? Why's that?'

Ellie explained Sylvia had found Penelope and felt guilty. If it didn't come out in their conversation, she would ask him where he had been when Penelope was killed, but they could knock on doors in Ripple and ask about.

'That right? I heard she's been arrested.'

'You'll be hearing she's been released soon enough,' Ellie countered. 'Do you have any idea who might've wanted Penelope dead? Who might have killed her, even?'

'Are you trying to ask me if I did?'

Ellie had got used to people saying this. It was as if asking them who might have wanted their relative dead made them feel defensive. 'Did you?'

'Do you think I'd admit it if I had?'

She smiled, playing along with the game. 'Of course not. I just wanted to see what you'd say. Perhaps you could answer my other question though. Any idea who might want her out of the way?'

'I'm sure you've done your digging.'

'We have. Can you think of anyone we might *not* have found? Anyone only *you* might know about?'

'I haven't been part of my wife's life for nearly ten years. I wasn't always the best husband – I worked long hours and was away a lot – but I loved her and tried to do the best for her.'

Ellie wanted to think about his comments but there wasn't time now.

'I have no idea what she's been up to in that time and I've no idea who she's involved with. You'd be better off speaking to our son. He and his mother have always been tight. The last time I saw her was at my sentencing hearing.'

'Thank you. I'd like to ask two further questions please. Is Beech Farm in both of your names?'

'No.'

'Could you enlighten me?'

'It had been jointly owned, but Penelope made me sign it over to her before I went to prison. She was rather annoyed with me.'

He clearly liked understatement.

'And who's her heir?' She had a feeling she knew what he was going to say.

'Who do you think? Penelope was determined to make life as difficult for me as possible.'

'You mean she wanted to punish you?'

'That's exactly what I mean.'

So, Felix could answer directly when he wanted to.

'Just to be clear: are you saying Zane was her sole heir?'

He glanced down at the next log and struck it smack-bang in the centre with the axe. 'You get it.'

Chapter 22

DS Carmichael handed Sylvia a cup of tea and a mini packet of custard creams.

'Following on from our interview earlier, in which we informed you a witness has claimed they saw you kill Penelope Wyndham, can I ask you again whether you did?'

Sylvia let out a sigh. 'I absolutely did *not* and anyone telling you that is fabricating it. They cannot have evidence because it did not happen. I can only assume someone is trying to set me up.' She paused. 'I know my rights. I'd like you to either charge me or release me.'

DS Carmichael shook her head. 'Can't do that, I'm afraid. There's more, unfortunately.'

Sylvia frowned.

'Are you sure you don't want legal advice?'

'Perfectly. I've done nothing wrong.'

The detective continued. 'The crime scene investigators found blood on the fairy lights that were used to kill Penelope. This blood matches familial DNA we have on our database.'

Sylvia gulped.

'Given the DNA on our system also links with *you*, it will be tested further against the samples taken when we arrested you, to see if it matches yours.'

Sylvia nodded.

'All police officers have their DNA tested and stored for elimination purposes,' DS Carmichael explained. 'Do you understand what this means?'

Chapter 23

'Eleanor,' came the familiar female voice.

There were only two people in the world – apart from doctors and dentists and officials – who used that name. One was Ellie's mother. The other was Sally's.

'I was just saying to my daughter the other day that I hope you and David get back together this Christmas.' She stood up and a hot water bottle slid to the floor. She was already in her pyjamas. 'What is it? Three years now?'

'It is. Hello, Mrs Jones.' Ellie crossed the lounge and gave her a hug. It made her smile that Sally's mother insisted on using Ellie's legal name, and she still called her 'Mrs Jones'. A strange and rather touching tradition.

It was a cosy room. Open fire roaring away in the hearth. Logs drying beside it. Curtains drawn and the TV on. The same carpet and curtains they'd always had.

'He's a good man. Don't let him slip through your fingers, will you?'

Sally popped her head round the door. 'Ignore Mum. She still thinks we're sixteen.'

Ellie smiled nostalgically. Going into Sally's house was like going home. Growing up, she'd spent as much time here, and at Dave's house, as at the windmill. She knew the building's anomalies. The tap that leaked in the downstairs toilet. The extra step at the top of the stairs. The boiler that didn't always start. The uneven tiles in the hall.

After half an hour of reminiscing, they got to talking about Katie Douglas and the Wyndhams.

'Sal said there was something you wanted to tell me?' Ellie prompted.

Sally's mother nodded. 'He was very handsome, you know.'

'Who, Mum?' asked Sally, who had joined them.

'Felix. Before he and Penelope got together, I used to date him.' She paused. 'But she was much more glamorous, of course, and he dropped me for her.'

Chapter 24

Ellie was sitting at the kitchen table, checking the oven timings for cooking the turkey on Christmas Day. Zoe sat next to her with her laptop open. They both had hair masks on and towels round their heads.

Something was tripping the fuse board at the windmill, so Finn had come for supper in exchange for a bit of help with the electrics, and Sarge had just joined them too, having been round to Hargrave's old family home.

'His mother died about ten years ago and his father sold up,' he told Ellie and Zoe as he hung up his coat and scarf. 'The new owners of the house don't know where he went.'

'What about siblings?' asked Zoe.

'Tried his sister but she hasn't heard from him in years.' His forehead was creased with worry. 'She's obviously seen the news reports about the murder at Mistletoe Manor and was concerned, so she's tried calling him, but his phone is switched off.'

'Makes sense if he's lying low,' Ellie replied. 'That way his location can't be tracked.'

'I'll keep putting out feelers,' Sarge continued. 'He might be hiding out somewhere. I hope he is. The alternative is... he's come to harm.' He closed his eyes and gently shook his head, as though the thought was too unbearable to consider.

'I suppose that's a possibility, isn't it?' said Ellie. 'If he saw who killed Penelope, for example, or knows who did it.'

Sarge joined Finn in the lounge, where he was running a new extension lead around the circular walls of the windmill to create a safer source of power for the lights on the tree.

'Can we have *Hark the Herald*, please?' Ellie asked Zoe. 'We all need a bit of cheering up.' She was watching Sarge; his head was low and his hands were in his pockets. He looked despondent.

'Did you and Dad decide not to go out this evening then?' Zoe asked. She tapped at her phone and the carol began playing.

'Your dad wanted to,' Ellie replied, 'but I don't feel comfortable about going out when there are safety issues here, and your gran's in custody.'

'I can understand that. I feel the same. I'd planned to pop into the pub for a bit of Finn's gig this afternoon, but I didn't feel like it.' She gave Ellie a kind smile. 'By the way, I've put your photos from the switching-on of the lights on my laptop so they're easier to see.'

'Are you saying my photography's rubbish?' Ellie teased.

'Nowhere near as bad as Gran's but I'll let you off. She refuses to use manual focus and doesn't wait long enough for auto. Her shots are always blurry.'

Ellie was sitting with her notepad. 'Right. If we're going to eat at 2pm on Christmas Day, the turkey will need to go in the oven at 7am. The bird needs to be out of the fridge for an hour beforehand, and the oven will take a good fifteen mins to heat up. So, someone needs to be up at 6am.'

'We'll all help, Mum. Set our alarms.' Zoe pointed at a photograph of her and Finn on their stilts. 'You did a good job coaching us,' she shouted over to Sarge. 'Especially with the snow.'

'Thank you,' he replied. 'Before my accident, I always loved walking on stilts. They weren't my act, but I'd regularly borrow them from my colleagues.'

'To start with, I was scared I'd fall.' Zoe stretched the touchscreen to zoom in, and chuckled. 'Although you might not think I was confident from the expression on my face. Look.' She nudged her mum.

'That's shock,' Ellie replied. 'It looks like something spooked you.'

'Hmm.'

'Are there any of Hargrave? I'd like to get a clearer image of his face in my mind.'

Zoe flicked through the photos.

'Wait,' exclaimed Ellie. 'That's *Felix*. Zoom in, lovey, please. He told me he wasn't at the lights on Thursday.' She was trying to think of explanations for Felix's inaccurate information.

Zoe enlarged the image. Clear as day, Felix was shown, drinking mulled wine and laughing, with a blonde woman. 'I'll text Dad. Has he got the hump with you, Mum, for cancelling on him again?'

'A bit. He's upset because it's his night off and he loves the cathedral carols. It's the last concert before Christmas.

But all I can think about is that your gran's probably been sitting on a hard seat for hours and is starving.'

Zoe tapped a message and pressed Send. 'The cathedral is special, I guess.' She changed the subject. 'Still, he's bound to be worried about Gran too.'

'Oh, he is. It's just that his way of relaxing is to distract himself whereas I feel better if I problem-solve and do something.' She sighed. 'Anyway – this photograph isn't evidence Felix murdered Penelope. But it *is* evidence he lied to me.'

Zoe's phone dinged. She swiped the screen and read the message. 'Dad's asked for a copy of the photo. I'll send it to him.'

Ellie smiled.

'I wonder if Felix lied to the cops too,' Finn added. 'On *TrueCrime* on Netflix, they said that's perverting the course of justice.'

'We'll see.' Ellie was casting her mind back to Felix's exact words. 'I asked him if he was at the lights switch-on and he said he'd been working; that Thursday was his day for Ripple, Great Mongeham if he had time.'

'That's wanting to give the impression he hadn't been at the lights *at all*,' Zoe replied. 'Surely, most people would say they'd been working but stopped off for fifteen minutes to see the lights switched on, and then went back to work?'

'Yeah, but this is Felix Wyndham we're talking about. He could barely bring himself to speak to me.' Ellie described the way he'd carried on splitting logs with his axe.

'And that's not meant to be intimidating? What a creep.'

Ellie chuckled. She was curious to know how Felix had been with the police. 'We need to have another look at his movements. Get a proper alibi from him this time.'

'Definitely.'

'While we're on the subject of Felix,' Ellie continued, '*he* said Zane is Penelope's heir and Zane said he thought Felix would be.'

'Hmm,' said Zoe. 'That's odd. Perhaps Penelope didn't discuss her will with either of them and, because they don't get on, they've both assumed the other will benefit. What d'you think?'

'That makes sense.'

They carried on looking at the photos of the lights until they found one of Hargrave.

'Here we are,' said Zoe.

They'd all seen him get out of the driver's side of the limo and open the back door for Penelope.

'What's that on his cheek?' asked Zoe. She enlarged the area on the image. 'Is that some kind of mark?'

Ellie leaned over the laptop screen. 'Looks like it. A graze, maybe? Can you screenshot it?'

'Yes,' Zoe replied. 'It's a cut.' She pointed. 'Got the beginnings of a scab.'

Ellie's phone beeped with a Google alert for the *Wootton Gazette*. 'Here we go,' she shouted over to the lounge. 'Bet this is Katie Douglas' piece following her "chat" with Sally's mum.' She swiped the screen of her phone and clicked on the link in her email.

Sarge came over, leaving Finn running the new extension cable.

Ellie read aloud: *'Children's author in Christmas-themed murder – cop's wife arrested.'*

'Oh, good grief,' said Sarge. 'What a terrible headline–'

'Click-bait, isn't it?' Zoe told him.

Sarge's eyebrows shot up. 'The reporter's simultaneously tried to make it sound festive *and* has managed to drag in poor Sylvia.'

'She's going to be mortified,' said Ellie. 'Where did Katie get the information from? Flipping woman. This leaking of developments to the newspaper has been going on for too long.' She continued reading. *'Beleaguered children's author, Penelope Wyndham, died on Thursday evening in a suspicious incident at her new home, Wootton Manor (known locally as "Mistletoe Manor"), after switching on the Christmas lights in Lower Wootton.'*

'Beleaguered?' Sarge muttered. 'I don't like the sound of that.'

'Right,' Ellie replied. 'You just know Katie is going to dredge up as much dirt as she can.' She carried on reading. *'Police are investigating the circumstances of Mrs Wyndham's death and appeal for information from anyone knowing what happened. The author retired recently, following a high-profile scandal in which she was accused of stealing a younger writer's work and following her husband's conviction for art fraud.'*

'I suppose she was bound to bring that up,' said Sarge.

Ellie gave a begrudging nod and carried on reading the article. 'That's strange. Look. Katie's mentioned the fairy lights. As far as I know, the *modus operandi* hasn't been released to the public yet, has it?'

'I haven't heard it mentioned,' Zoe replied.

'On *TrueCrime*, they're always saying how unhelpful it is to leak the M.O.,' Finn shouted over from the lounge. 'And that it can result in copycat murders.'

'Dad isn't going to be pleased.'

'It's also deliberately perverting the course of justice, as it'll interfere with the police's questioning,' Finn added.

Ellie reverted to the article. *'Her death comes after the troubled author announced plans for a comeback for her popular children's adventure series. In a bizarre twist, the wife of the late Detective Inspector Ronald Blix, and mother of Detective Inspector Dave Blix, was arrested on Saturday morning and remains in custody.'* Ellie groaned.

Sarge had joined them. 'That makes poor Sylvia sound really guilty.'

Zoe spun round to face her mum. 'Why are the police still holding her? Surely they've got to explain why they arrested her?'

'It doesn't work like that,' Ellie explained. 'You know that. If someone has testified against your gran, they have to investigate. If her DNA evidence is around the body, even more so.'

The annoying thing was they didn't know the basis for the arrest. They were just guessing.

'They're bound to have her DNA evidence there,' said Zoe. '*She* found Penelope.'

Sarge stared first at Ellie then Zoe.

'Your mum's right,' said Finn. 'The police can't just dismiss eye witness testimony, if they have it, and forensic evidence. They need to piece together what happened, who was involved and the precise sequence of events. And that takes time.'

'I wonder who else's DNA was at the crime scene?' Ellie asked, her mind buzzing with questions. 'Presumably whoever else has been in that part of the Great Hall. Some from people you'd expect to find there, like Hargrave and her son, if he's visited.'

'And the killer,' Zoe added.

There was a loud CLICK, and the lights and music went off.

'Fuse board's tripped,' said Sarge. 'Where is it?'

'It's above the back door,' Ellie told him, and he shuffled over.

'Our electricity's gone off,' Nigel shouted over the banisters from upstairs. 'Hope it wasn't me boiling the kettle?'

'It'll be back on in a minute,' Ellie yelled up. 'Can you unplug everything?' She went back over to Zoe. 'I'm very suspicious of Hargrave. It's odd that he disappeared just when Penelope was killed. I can't help wondering if it was *him* claiming Sylvia murdered Penelope? I can't see how it can be anyone else.'

'That should do it,' said Sarge, looking rather pleased with himself as he rejoined them.

The lights came back on. *Hark the Herald* resumed, then: CLICK.

'Oh, for goodness' sake,' snapped Ellie. 'There must be an appliance it doesn't like.'

'We'll need to isolate everything,' Sarge told them.

Zoe gave her mum an anxious look.

'It's alright. He did some of the electrics at the circus,' Ellie informed her, hoping for the best.

The three of them went round the ground floor, unplugging everything.

'I'll nip upstairs,' said Ellie. 'See what Bridget and Nigel have got plugged in.'

As she padded up the stairs, Ellie thought about Felix. Could his acrimonious relationship with his wife be a useful cover? What if he'd been deliberately telling people he hadn't seen her for years when really he'd nipped into the manor house and strangled her?

Upstairs now, Ellie knocked on the door to Zoe's old room. 'Something's tripping the consumer unit.' She glanced in and her eyes fell on the kettle and a set of hair straightening irons which were loaded onto a multi-socket adapter.

An adapter which *they* must've brought with them because the Blixes never used them...

Nearby, on Zoe's desk, Ellie's iron was cooling down. They must have borrowed it from the kitchen.

'Er... would it be OK to plug those into separate sockets?' she asked, pointing, determined not to apologise. She felt like directing them to the Guest Information sheet on the back of the door. 'It's an old building and they're all high voltage.' She hoped they'd get the message and not write a review on TripAdvisor saying the electrics were unsafe. 'If you've finished with the iron, I'll take it back downstairs. There's an ironing board there if you want to use it next time.'

Nigel nodded.

Back in the kitchen a few minutes later, she returned to Katie's article, and they regrouped. She began reading aloud again from the newspaper.

'Brand new evidence suggests that Felix's conviction wasn't the only skeleton the Wyndhams had in their closet.'

'Oh, crikey,' Sarge muttered. 'What else has that woman unearthed?'

'Here at the Wootton Gazette, we have seen evidence that Felix Wyndham not only had an affair, but he also had a daughter...'

Ellie looked at Zoe. 'Surely it's got to be–'

'Rebecca Wyndham,' Zoe screeched.

Implications were darting through Ellie's mind.

'Dad must know. I'll text him though, just in case.'

'So, when Rebecca told us she's Penelope's daughter, she meant *step-daughter*.'

'I didn't think this case could get any crazier,' Zoe added.

Ellie read the last paragraph of the article. *'Only child Zane Wyndham isn't an only child after all, and now we need to factor half-sister Rebecca into the mix. All we can say is: watch this space. By the time we report again, will*

Sylvia Blix have been released? If not, how will the village source frangipane mince pies? Will half-siblings Zane and Rebecca be making wreaths togeth–'

'That's it,' said Ellie. 'That's where I know her from. Sally and I booked a wreath-making workshop with her a couple of months ago. I couldn't go in the end as I had to help a B&B guest who'd sprained their ankle, but Sal went. It was in Rebecca's garden studio in Martin Mill and I remember her picture from the website. She sent me her business card when she refunded me.' She scuttled over to her bag, fished out her wallet and produced a card. 'Here we are. Becky Norton. The Wreath Company.'

'I guess Norton might be her biological mother's name, or a married name,' said Zoe. She glanced back to the webpage. 'The article finishes with... "*And if the butler didn't do it – clue: there is no butler – what about the missing chauffeur? Or was he too busy stealing the silver?*"'

'What is she talking about, "stealing the silver"?' said Sarge, an indignant tone in his voice.

'I've no idea but I've heard enough,' said Ellie, a determined set to her jaw. 'We must get to the bottom of this death once and for all.' She stood up, hands on hips.

'And – I want to know why Zane told us the only Rebecca he knows is the one who works for him.'

Chapter 25

Ellie took the top off the biscuit tin, changed her mind and replaced it. She'd picked at her supper. Sylvia had been in custody for ten hours and it was getting late.

'Mum?' Zoe's voice was tight with anxiety.

'It's nine o'clock. I can't sit here doing nothing, not knowing if they're going to let her go home this evening.' Ellie stood up, sending her chair screeching backwards on the floor.

Rebus raised his head.

'I've got to do something to move this investigation on.' She paced across the kitchen to the tap, filled a glass and drained it. 'I hate the idea of your gran having to spend the night in custody.'

Zoe picked up her phone. 'Shall I text Dad and–?'

'No. It won't make any difference. They've got to go through their procedures. It's just the waiting... Your poor gran. I hope they've given her some proper food.' Ellie faced Zoe, her eyes blazing. 'Can you stay here in case the police station rings? If the lanes aren't blocked, I'm going to drive over to Rebecca's. See what she's got to say for herself.'

From the main road out of Lower Wootton, Ellie turned left into Mill Road. It was downhill and the snow was fresh, and the jeep's large wheels made easy work of it for around a mile. Then, as the road narrowed, becoming Buttermilk Lane, the snow was much thicker, and the wheels started to spin and falter. The jeep careered from one side of the lane to the other.

Perhaps this hadn't been a good idea. Should she turn back and go home? What if Rebecca wasn't even at home? If Ellie got stuck, her car breakdown service wouldn't thank her for venturing out in such treacherous conditions.

She kept going slowly, creeping along in the jeep and finally arrived. Ellie recognised the property from when she'd come to book the wreath-making workshop. It was a pretty, thatched cottage which sat behind a white picket fence. Rendered and painted white, it glowed in the moonlight and the reflection off the snow.

Downstairs, lights were on and in an upstairs room, a light illuminated dark curtains from within.

She opened the wooden gate, picked her way up the snowy path, rang the bell and waited.

The woman who opened the door was the same one who'd come round to the windmill earlier in the week. This time she was in her dressing gown and slippers, a deep frown across her forehead, mousey hair tied up in a top knot.

'Sorry to... er... turn up so late,' said Ellie. 'My mother-in-law is in custody and we're all very worried.' She changed tack. 'I'm not sure if you're Becky Norton from The Wreath Company or Penelope Wyndham's stepdaughter, Rebecca?'

'I use "Becky" and "Norton" is my married name,' Rebecca replied. "Rebecca" is just for forms and legal stuff.' She paused. 'I introduced myself to you guys as "Rebecca Wyndham" as that's the name on my birth certificate. I'm sorry I was so rude. I've had... er... a complicated relationship with Penelope and Felix and was thrown into a panic that it was going to all come out.'

Ellie registered her answer. 'That's sort of what's brought me here. We saw the article in the local newspaper.'

Her eyes filled with tears. 'We've just seen it too. It's exactly what I wanted to avoid. I guess I was being naïve.'

'Katie Douglas dredges up awful stuff on people. It's not local news. It's gossip.' Ellie paused. 'When you came round on Thursday, why didn't you tell us you're Felix's daughter?'

She sighed and her voice took on a tone of profound sadness. 'Not telling people about him has been the story of my life.' She pulled the door in, allowing Ellie to enter the house.

Ellie stepped into a lounge with a tree, and presents, and a lamp glowing softly on a coffee table. A wood-burning stove was blazing away. On a sheepskin rug by the hearth, a black cat was purring and kneading the wool beneath its paws.

'D'you want a seat?' She gestured to the sofa and shuffled towards an armchair.

Ellie sat down.

'My husband's upstairs with the children. It was his turn for the bedtime story tonight.' She chuckled affectionately.

'It goes on for over an hour when he does it. They refuse to go to sleep so they can keep him reading.' She smiled then frowned, as though she realised she'd lost her train of thought.

'I was asking about Felix.'

'Oh, yeah.' She seemed to reconnect with her feelings. 'All my life, I've either not known Felix was my dad or had to keep it secret. You see – Felix and Penelope didn't want anyone to know about his affair with my mum...'

'Ah.'

'And, therefore, didn't want anyone knowing about *me*.' Her eyes closed, as though even thinking about it caused her pain. 'My mother was young when she had me and wasn't able to keep me.'

'Where did she meet Felix, then?'

'At the tennis club apparently.'

Ellie's stomach lurched.

'She was partnering another lad at the time in doubles, and Felix was partnering Penelope. Apparently, Felix took a shine to her.'

This was hard to take in. Ellie's thoughts were racing and her conversation with Sally's mum came to mind. She hadn't mentioned anything about the tennis club, but could *she* be Becky's mother? She'd said Felix had dropped her for Penelope. Might they have continued seeing each other after Felix and Penelope were married?

'Have you had contact with her, then?'

Becky nodded. 'She provided a brief statement about the circumstances of my adoption but was adamant she didn't want to have any contact.' Her eyes brimmed with tears.

'That must be very hard. I'm so sorry.' Ellie decided against asking the woman's name. Unless it had a bearing on the case, it was nobody's business except the people involved.

Becky wiped tears away with the back of her hand. 'My adoptive parents didn't want me to trace my birth parents. They were worried about me getting hurt all over again.'

'That's understandable,' Ellie said softly.

'When I did, they supported my decision but when I found out he was Felix Wyndham, they weren't keen on me going public about it either.'

Ellie felt a rush of sympathy for Becky.

'My adoptive parents are lovely people. I've been very lucky with them. They've only ever wanted the best for me.'

As Ellie waited for Becky to decide what she wanted to say, she sensed the love in this pretty cottage and was pleased the young woman had experienced that from her adoptive parents.

'Before I knew my biological mother had given me up, I thought my family was like everyone else's. I called them Mum and Dad – because that's what they were.' She swallowed. 'But everything changed when I found out. And the rejection – which I didn't know had happened – started to affect me.'

Becky looked around the room, as if she was searching for anchors.

'In some ways, I wish I'd never started the process. I should've taken Mum and Dad's advice and let sleeping dogs lie.'

The cat got up, arched its back in a long stretch and sauntered over to its owner.

'Felix had never told Penelope about his affair. I had counselling before I submitted the application and learnt that, when a new partner doesn't know about a child from a previous relationship, the chances of being accepted by the biological parent's new family are greatly reduced.' A hollow laugh erupted from her. 'That was an understatement.' She stroked the cat. 'Penelope hated me. Felix was pleased to meet me and wanted to get to know me...' She turned to Ellie. 'That made Penelope hate me even more.' She paused, as though she was deciding how much to share. 'And it's fair to say the feeling was completely mutual.'

'I'm so sorry.' Ellie was trying to understand what must've been competing desires and drives. These revelations gave Becky a potential motive to want Penelope out of the way. She could see how Becky might want to get revenge on the woman who'd rejected her and refused to acknowledge her into the family. She saw also how Becky might want to remove a threat source from her life in the area.

But Ellie also couldn't help thinking about Sally's mother. She would have to park that issue for now. She hadn't wanted to be made privy to the information, and it wasn't hers to dig around in. She would think later about what to do with it – after all, it was by no means definitely her who'd given Becky up. 'What about Zane?'

She groaned. 'He could see how his mother felt and that was his primary concern. They've always been extremely close.'

That was the second time they'd heard that.

'He's never got on with Felix,' Becky continued, 'so I don't think it bothered him that Felix wanted to have a relationship with me, but he was adamant – like my biological mother – that he didn't want anything to do with me.'

Was that why Zane had denied knowing anyone called Rebecca? It seemed plausible. She wasn't going to tell Becky this was what he'd done. It would probably upset her further.

Ellie was wondering how things stood with wills and legacies when a new family member was revealed. She wasn't sure whether to ask and decided to wait and see what else came out in their conversation.

Another question popped into her mind: why had Penelope's rental of Mistletoe Manor been in Rebecca's name? She began with some basic questions first, trying to stay away from anything too sensitive. 'How did you find out Penelope had died?'

'The police came round. I assume Zane told them about me. They said a woman had found her body; someone who'd been helping with preparations for the party. I guessed it was your mother-in-law as Felix said she'd been helping Penelope. I think she'd been in the kitchen when he went round one time.'

'When did you last see Penelope?'

She pursed her lips. 'At the switching on of the lights, along with everyone else.' She rolled her eyes. 'I didn't want to go – for obvious reasons – but the children did, so my husband and I said we'd go for an hour and make sure we avoided contact with her.'

'And before that?' Ellie's phone started to vibrate in her pocket.

'When our youngest was born. Penelope somehow found out and demanded to see him. Turned up here, spouting what she perceived were her grandmother's rights.'

'Wasn't that a bit weird? She didn't want a relationship with you, but she did with your child?'

Tension gripped the muscles in Becky's face. 'Thank you. That was my view. Perhaps she sees grandchildren differently. I have no idea.'

'Presumably, she saw Zane's girls regularly?'

'Think so. They were all happy families, as far as I can gather.'

'What did you decide about your youngest?'

'I talked it over with my husband and told her: no.'

'How did that go down?'

'Not well at all. She was furious. Sent me a horrible letter via her solicitor, demanding access.'

'And has that been resolved?'

Ellie's phone vibrated again.

Becky shook her head. 'I didn't reply.'

'What about Felix? Have you continued to see him?'

She nodded. 'Quietly. And staying away from Lower Wootton.' A faint smile spread over her face. 'Quite a bit more since he came out of prison.' She looked Ellie in the eye. 'I know a lot of people don't like him and I've felt conflicted where he's concerned. He might be weak, but he's got a good heart.'

This was what the vicar had said – the last part anyway.

A single tear rolled down Becky's cheek. 'Deep down, all Felix wants is to keep people happy.'

Ellie sensed she wasn't finished.

'You do know that the art fraud was Penelope's idea, not Felix's, don't you?'

Chapter 26

Ellie left Becky's cottage with her head full of questions. Could Felix's affair with Becky's mother be related to Penelope's murder? Might Becky be involved? She decided to catch up with Zane in the morning and get his side of the story.

She swiped her phone as she walked to the car. There were six missed calls: three from Zoe, two from Dave and one from the police station.

She selected Dave's number and pressed Dial.

'Hey. Mum can go home.'

'Oh-h.' She let out a sigh. 'Thank goodness.'

'I'm on my way to pick her up now. Shall I bring her back to the windmill?'

'Please.'

'She's been released pending further investigation, so she's not out of the woods yet, but it's obviously much better than them applying for an extension to keep her in custody.'

'OK. Zoe's at home. I'm just... um... on my way back.'

'Where've you been? We've been calling you for the last fifteen minutes.'

'I went to see Becky Wyndham. I'll tell you about it when you get to the house.'

Dave's Audi was on the drive when Ellie got home. She turned off Pennypot Lane and parked beside his car. For a moment, it felt liked old times...

The front door flew open, and Zoe came charging out, followed by Rebus. 'Mum!' Her face was blotchy. 'I've been phoning you but got no answer. Thought you'd got stuck in a snowdrift.'

'Sorry. I didn't hear it ringing.' She put her hand on Zoe's back. 'Let's go in. How's your gran?'

Zoe recounted her grandmother's stories of a custody sergeant with bad breath, stale bread and sweaty, processed cheese.

Sylvia was on the sofa with Leonard one side of her and Rebus, who'd jumped up, on the other.

Ellie knelt on the floor.

'It was a woman.' Sylvia threw a look at Dave.

'What was?' asked Ellie.

'A woman rang into the murder investigation team...' She paused, her voice shaking with anger, 'and said she saw me strangle Penelope after a row.'

Ellie turned to face Dave. 'Is this true?'

He nodded.

'Who was it?'

'We don't know yet.' He rubbed the stubble on his chin. 'We haven't been able to trace her.' Tiredness creased his forehead. It must've been stressful for him, having his mother in custody.

'Was that it? Did you arrest her just for that?'

Sylvia shook her head. 'They found my blood on the fairy lights that were used to strangle Penelope.'

Ellie's mouth gaped.

'Don't worry,' Sylvia added quickly. 'It was from when I helped Penelope to put up the tree and decorate it.'

'Thank goodness,' squealed Zoe.

'One of the glass baubles was broken in the box,' Sylvia continued, 'and I put my hand on it. Wasn't serious but it bled quite a bit. Hargrave got me some antiseptic spray and a plaster.'

Chapter 27 Day 4 SUNDAY

The following morning, Ellie was woken up by a hammering on the front door.

She shifted the kittens and got out of bed, padding downstairs in her pyjamas, Rebus dashing ahead, barking, while the insistent rapping continued.

She opened up to Sarge in black clothes and a beanie.

It was still dark.

'Good grief. Have you been out doing burglaries or something?'

'I think I know where Greg is,' he told her breathlessly, ignoring her remark.

For a moment, Ellie had forgotten that 'Greg' was Hargrave's real name.

'Can you get dressed? We need to go. I'm worried about him.'

A few minutes later Ellie was back at the door, in jeans and jumper, and was pulling on her coat, hat, scarf and walking boots. Sylvia hadn't stirred yet, so she left a note saying she'd be back shortly.

'He's a proud man. He would have hated the idea of people thinking he was a murderer.'

Sarge's loyalty to his childhood friend was admirable but Ellie wasn't sure she saw Greg in the same terms. She was worried that Sarge was biased. However, he was an intelligent man and certainly no fool, so Ellie owed him respect, and that meant at least keeping her mind open to his ideas and hunches.

'Do we need the jeep? Where are we going?'

'The allotments near Appledown Woods. When we were kids, his parents had a plot with a tiny shed. I'm pretty sure it's still there. We would often go and camp out there during school holidays and at weekends. It was his happy place.'

It was minus one degrees and snowing. An uninsulated allotment shed was not going to be anyone's idea of fun. But she would keep that thought to herself.

'OK, let's jump in the jeep. It'll be quicker and warmer.' She pulled on her gloves and began wiping the snow off her windscreen and windows, Sarge helping too.

The snow was thicker on Pennypot Lane, but they reached the allotments in a few minutes, parking behind a battered pickup. Ahead, a path led down to the allotments, a sunken area the size of a football pitch, which had been bombed during WWII.

Sarge pointed. 'That's their patch, by the wall.'

A tiny shed lay on the edge of the plot.

'Why wouldn't Greg go to his family, though?' asked Ellie.

He didn't answer.

Ellie felt torn. They needed to find Greg but, at the same time, she hoped he hadn't been kipping in a tin shed in freezing temperatures.

They clomped down the path and through the snow.

Sarge turned to Ellie, placing his finger to his lips in a request for silence. He pointed to a rickety, black bike with a basket which was leaning up against a wheelbarrow, presumably suggesting that it was Greg's. Sarge positioned himself outside the shed door. 'Greg?' he shouted. 'Mate, are you here?'

No answer.

Sarge pulled the door open and peered in.

Ellie came up behind him.

'No-one's here,' he said in a dejected voice.

They bundled in for a closer inspection, searching for signs he had been there. Tucked under a wooden worktop, someone had made a bed from old blankets and a sleeping bag. To the side was a holdall.

'He's been here,' said Sarge. 'That's his keyring.' He gestured to a bundle of keys on a ring with an English Heritage fob. 'He's had it for years.'

'Wonder where he's gone,' said Ellie. 'Somewhere warmer?'

'I'd imagine so.'

'Right. We can sit in my car with the heater on and wait for him to come back, or we can try all the places he might be able to get into at night. Or for food, a shower.'

'Let's look for him. The Rattling Cat and the Windmill Inn are open late, and warm. He could've hidden somewhere when they called last orders. Got away with staying there.'

'Yep,' Ellie replied. 'And the private gym by the garage has showers.' It was the first thing she thought of. 'They're open 'til late and it's pretty quiet in winter. Maybe he snuck in.'

Sarge was rubbing his stubble. 'There are public loos near the library. Not very warm but less draughty than the shed.'

'I think they're locked at night. What about outhouses and barns? There are plenty at Beech Farm. Would he go there, with Zane staying there?'

'Doubt it,' said Sarge gruffly. 'There's also Mistletoe Manor. That's got plenty of barns. Although I doubt he'd go back there with the police, and Zane and us, tramping in and out.'

'You know him. Which place d'you think is most likely?'

'I'd say the gym. He can get supplies from the garage.'

'They don't open 'til midday so he'd be able to leave without anyone discovering him.' Ellie knew this, as Finn and Charlie used their facilities. 'However, he's unlikely to have both the keys and alarm code.'

'I've got another idea,' Sarge said. 'When we were growing up, Greg's aunt had a home on a holiday park at St Margaret's. A caravan on stilts, basically. Everyone in his family used it. It was like an overfill place at Christmas and

Easter when lots of family members wanted to come and stay at the seaside, and there wasn't room at the house.'

'Do you think he might be there? Do they still have their plot?'

'I don't know. It was a long time ago but I'm sure he will have realised that a lot of those homes lie empty, particularly in the winter.'

'Shall we take a drive round there and see if we can find him? If he's been staying at the gym, I can't see how we're going to get in. He must have to hide out somewhere, allow himself to be locked in for the night and escape as soon as the staff arrive. So, we can't do anything until then.'

'Good idea. It's early still so it shouldn't be too hard to figure out which caravans are occupied and which are empty.'

They were quickly winding their way through the pretty village of St Margaret's, past the section by the church where the road narrowed with buildings either side. Then up the hill, past the farm, and into the road that ran through wide open fields.

They drove over a speed hump into the holiday park. Ellie spotted some parking by the side of the road.

'I'm going to stop here. If we start driving round the grounds, we're bound to come up on someone's security camera and get stopped.'

She squeezed the jeep in between a plumber's van and a Range Rover.

The two of them got out.

Ellie scanned the site. It was a combination of park homes and single-storey, brick buildings with flat roofs.

'Their caravan was at the side near the lane we've just driven along,' Sarge said, his voice a whisper. 'It had views over the bay and the Channel. Let's walk down that way first. My guess is that's what he would have done.'

They trudged through the snow in the early morning light. Ellie felt a sense of trepidation. Were they going to find Greg? If so, what would he tell them?

'Down here,' Sarge told her. 'If I remember correctly, it was about the third or fourth on the right.' He peered at every home. 'That one's got people in... motorbike outside that one... light on over there.' There was a dull thudding of music. 'Not that one... curtains drawn on the big one with the veranda.'

He stopped. 'Oh. It's gone.' He cast about. 'Theirs was here along with five or six others, but they've moved them and made this bit into a launderette.' He continued surveying the scene. 'If he's here, he's either going to be camping out somewhere warmish, like the launderette, or staying in a home that's not being used.'

'I was going to suggest the launderette, but I can't see anyone sleeping there. It would only take someone with insomnia who goes to do their laundry early and raises the alarm, and Greg would be found out.'

'I agree. He wouldn't risk that. He's more likely to slope along the hedge and sneak into one of the homes here.' He pointed at a dense privet hedge and traced his finger along a line of vans on the horizon.

They inched forward, trying to be as quiet as possible. Somewhere in the distance a dog barked.

'Would he draw the curtains?' Ellie whispered. 'If the owners aren't staying there, and the curtains aren't usually pulled across, surely that would just attract attention to the site staff and other guests?'

'I agree. He'd want to make himself as invisible as possible. Put something over his eyes to keep the light out. That's what I'd do.' He took a few more steps.

'What about this one?' said Ellie. 'Doesn't look like anyone's here legitimately.' She approached a window and peered in, then shifted along to the next window and the one after that.

Sarge gestured to another home and went to look in the windows there. Both of those drew a blank and they moved on.

'Psst,' Sarge hissed a few moments later. He waved his arms, beckoning. He pointed at one window in particular, whispering, 'There's a solid mass on the floor which could easily be someone sleeping.'

Ellie nodded. 'What shall we do? Knock on the window? Try the door?' Her heart was thumping, and the hairs were standing up on the back of her neck.

'Let me see if I can get a better look,' said Sarge. 'If I'm sure it's him, I don't mind trying the door and going in, if it's open. But I don't want to walk in on a stranger. They might have a dog or...'

Ellie shuddered.

Sarge pushed his face up close to the window.

Ellie wasn't sure what Greg might be wearing. Even if he'd left his job in a hurry, or been sacked, he would presumably have changed out of his chauffeur's uniform into his own clothes. But what those might be, she had no idea.

Sarge was on tiptoe. 'Whoever it is, they've definitely got dark hair, which Sarge has. Bit difficult to see what the build might be. The time before last when I saw him, he was wearing a long, black winter coat.' He stood back for Ellie to look. 'What do you think?'

She screwed up her eyes. 'He's definitely wearing dark clothes, but I can't see much more than that, I'm afraid. Why don't we tap on the window and see if he wakes up? If he sees you, he won't be scared.'

'And if it's not him?'

Ellie shrugged. 'Apologise and explain, I guess. Let's cross that bridge if we come to it.' Unless the person in the park home had collapsed, it was most likely they were there unofficially too, so hopefully there wouldn't be any complaints.

Sarge tapped on the window, quietly at first then a bit louder.

The person on the floor shifted and raised their head.

'Greg, mate, it's me, Sarge.' He waved. 'Can you let us in?'

A few moments later, the caravan door creaked open. 'Have you got the cops with you?' Greg's voice trembled as he surveyed the scene.

'No,' Sarge replied. 'We're here to get you help. We're worried about you.'

Greg sank down onto the floor of the caravan with a moan of relief.

An hour later they were all back in the kitchen at the windmill, having collected Greg's bag from the shed at the allotment. He'd had a shower, changed his clothes and scoffed a bacon sandwich.

'What happened?' Sarge asked him finally. 'Why did you leave Mistletoe Manor?'

Ellie was leaving the questioning to Sarge.

'Penelope accused me of stealing.' He covered his face with his hands.

This is what the local paper had reported.

'Stealing what?' Ellie asked.

'First of all, it was cash from her bag, then housekeeping money from a drawer in the kitchen.' His voice was barely audible. 'Then she started saying I was stealing things from the house. Silver, cut glass, an expensive clock. It was too much.' He lowered his head. 'I've never stolen *anything* from anyone. I can only think that she wanted to get rid of me. Figured the only way to do that was to make trouble for me with the Selby family.’

Ellie couldn’t stay silent. ‘I’m sorry. That’s wrong.’

‘Unfortunately,’ said Sarge in a grave voice, ‘you going AWOL has made people wonder what else you might be guilty of.’ He gave Ellie an accusatory look.

She held her hands palm up in a gesture of admission. ‘It did make me wonder. But I wasn’t the only one.' She faced Greg. 'I don’t know you like Sarge does, and it’s our job to ask questions.’

Greg gave an understanding nod. ‘I don’t blame you. I’m sure everyone’s been saying I killed her. But I didn’t. I wouldn’t be so stupid.’ He stared into the distance, gently shaking his head. ‘I’ve worked for the Selbys my whole life. Had *one* job. What am I going to do? Almost all my adult life I’ve lived at Mistletoe Manor.’

‘I’m sure the family will give you your job back,’ Sarge told his friend. ‘They’ll know you won’t have stolen anything. Once Penelope’s murder is solved, everything will blow over.’

Ellie blurted: ‘If items have gone missing, there will be an explanation. They’ll be found and returned.’

Sarge nodded. 'Speaking of Penelope's death,' he said, 'do you know what happened? Were you still there then?'

'No,' said Greg. 'When I left her, she was very much alive. But she'd started on at me in the limo on the way back to the house. Said I'd taken a set of silver fish cutlery that had disappeared.'

Sarge tutted.

'She'd already accused me of nicking it and I'd told her I hadn't.' He sighed. 'Simply wouldn't accept what I was saying.'

'What happened?' Sarge rubbed his chin.

'I lost my patience with her.' He touched the bruise on his cheek. 'She'd thrown a glass ashtray at me before we set off for the lights. So, when we got back to the manor house afterwards, she resumed her accusations and I told her I'd had enough. I was leaving.'

Ellie tutted. 'That's dreadful. What did she expect?'

Greg shrugged.

'You didn't see anyone at that point?' asked Sarge. 'No guests arriving early for the soirée at the manor house? Or family members turning up?'

'No. Neither. No-one. I knew Sylvia was due on foot, but she hadn't arrived. I didn't like Penelope, but had I seen anything remotely threatening towards her, I would have got her help. It was my job to make sure she was safe, if you like. It's what the Selbys were paying me to do.'

'Have the police spoken to you?' Ellie asked.

He shook his head. 'I've been... hiding. I haven't wanted to speak to anyone.'

Ellie nodded. 'You'll need to talk to them now though. You might have information which could help their investigation.'

'Where are you going to stay?' Sarge asked. 'You can't sleep in the shed at the allotment. It's too cold. And you can't carry on sleeping at the holiday park either.'

Greg shrugged.

'We don't have any spare rooms here at the windmill but you're welcome to stay in our outhouse. I've got a plug-in electric heater we could put in there for you? It *is* insulated at least.'

'Alternatively,' said Sarge, 'I haven't got Sean living with me anymore and have plenty of room at my house. You're welcome to stay there.'

'That's very kind of both of you. I'll definitely take one of you up on your offer.'

'Can I check one further thing, please?' said Ellie. 'Were you at the house when Sylvia cut her finger on a Christmas bauble?'

He nodded. 'I brought her a plaster and some of that spray stuff from the first aid box. Antiseptic.'

That was a relief. Hopefully, it would clear things up with the police once and for all.

'Morning,' came two voices at the bottom of the stairs.

Nigel was rubbing his hands and grinning as he and Bridget approached. 'I've been thinking about your delicious sausages for the last hour. How long will breakfast be?'

Chapter 28

Having checked the Blix Blitz diary, Ellie cooked a bumper breakfast for the B&B guests, plus Greg, Sarge and Zoe. Half an hour later, she stacked the crockery and pans in the dishwasher and rang Zane to ask if he could meet them at Mistletoe Manor with the keys. She wanted to see Penelope's bedroom again and ask Zane about Becky.

Ellie and Sarge left Sylvia playing cards with Greg at the kitchen table.

As they pulled up on the drive outside Mistletoe Manor, the front door opened, and Zane appeared. 'Morning,' he shouted over, his hand raised in a greeting.

'He must've seen the newspaper article, surely?' muttered Sarge.

'If he hasn't, he's going to get a shock.' Ellie had been mulling over what to say to him.

They walked up the steps.

'I went to see your sister last night,' she said, carefully observing Zane's expression. 'Becky.'

His face fell. 'Ah.' He blushed and led her into the hall.

'Well, it's no secret now,' Sarge said, following Ellie in. 'I assume you've seen the article in the local paper?'

He nodded.

Ellie continued: 'You told me the only Rebecca you know is one of your staff.'

'Yeah,' he replied in an embarrassed voice. 'To start with, when you asked me the question, I wasn't thinking about my half-sister because Dad's always called her "Becky". My PR assistant *is* the only other Rebecca I know, and she was who I thought of, if that makes sense.'

'Becky is the name she uses,' Ellie said, noting his reluctance to refer to her as his sister.

'I was about to ask if you meant my half-sister when I realised more than anything I wanted to protect my mother's memory. To delay people knowing about my father's affair and the daughter that resulted. So, I let the denial remain.'

'It was going to come out in either the police investigation or ours.'

'I know. I realised that as soon as I'd said it.'

'I even showed you her Facebook profile.'

'I think once I'd denied things, I felt like I had to continue with it. What's it called in business? Sunk cost fallacy, or something.'

Ellie frowned.

'It's where you've invested in something that's not going to work, but you keep going.' He threw his hands up in the air and looked her in the eye. 'It was a bit like that. What can I say? I genuinely meant well.'

It made sense and seemed honourable enough. She waited to see if he was going to comment further, but he'd begun sorting through the post.

'If you want us to help find your mother's killer, you need to be honest with us.' Ellie made sure her voice was firm. 'Do we have a deal?'

'Definitely. Sorry.' His shoulders sank sheepishly. He folded a couple of envelopes and stuffed them into his coat pocket.

Ellie changed the subject and asked if they could see Penelope's bedroom.

A few minutes later, she and Sarge were on the landing at the top of the stairs.

'Come on,' said Ellie. 'Quickly. This place gives me the creeps.' She led him into the bedroom.

The first thing she did was walk from the door to the bay window to look out onto the drive below, before turning and facing the room with her back to the light.

Penelope's bed.

Bedside cabinets.

Two freestanding wardrobes. Dressing table. Chest of drawers.

The wardrobe.

'That's it,' Ellie told Sarge. 'Sylvia said, when she came in here, Penelope's outfit was on a hanger on the back of the wardrobe door, shoes on the floor underneath it, and a fascinator. She must've been planning to change into it for the party. So, where's the outfit?'

'Would the police have put it away?'

'Doubt it,' she replied.

'Might they have taken it with them?' asked Sarge.

'Possibly but unlikely, I think. What information could it yield? She wasn't wearing it when she died. No, someone must've put it away. And that begs the questions–'

'Who – and why?'

She tiptoed over to the door and pushed it shut, not wanting Zane to get curious and come and disturb them. 'You try that one.' She pointed to the wardrobe to the left of the chimney breast. 'I'll try this one.' She pulled the door open and stood facing rows of outfits on hangers. 'Blimey. She liked her clothes. How on earth could she have worn all these?'

Sylvia had said it was a white dress.

Ellie parted each hanger from the next and examined the outfit and colour. 'Nope. Not here.'

Sarge was working more slowly so Ellie joined him at the other wardrobe, quickly spotting a long white dress.

'Here we are,' she said. 'Now, where are her shoes? We're looking for white stilettos.' She knelt down on the floor. The footwear in this wardrobe was all dark colours: black, brown, navy blue and grey. She tried the other wardrobe. Penelope didn't have many white shoes, so this part was easier. The stilettos were right at the front.

Ellie sat back, chewing thoughtfully at her lips.

'Something's not right here. Sylvia was adamant no-one was in the house when she got here. So, either someone's tidied up after the police left and handed over the crime scene–'

'That can only have been Zane,' said Sarge, 'so we can check that with him.'

'... or someone was here all the time, and they put away Penelope's outfit. Which do we think is the most likely?'

Sarge shrugged.

'I don't know either. But we can think more about that later. There's one item of her outfit that's still missing. The fascinator.'

'I'm not familiar with women's clothes and wardrobes,' said Sarge, 'but it seems she had different places for dresses, shoes, blouses. Where would she put fascinators?'

Ellie scanned the room.

The chest of drawers.

She pulled out each drawer and parted the items. No sign of the fascinator.

'Might she have kept a few things in one of the guest bedrooms?' asked Sarge.

'It's worth checking. There's no dressing table in here. Perhaps she does her hair and make-up somewhere else.'

The room next-door was smaller. Unlike Hargrave's room, here the bed had been covered by a throw. Three white cushions lay up against the headboard. Bedside table and lamp. A single wardrobe with drawers at the bottom. A dressing table was part of a full-length wooden unit which had cupboards around it, and a lower section you could sit at with a large mirror at the back.

Ellie spotted a black, bristle hairbrush, like the one her mother used. Next to it was a bottle of perfume. She recognised the distinctive square bottle with a pretend stopper for a lid. Amber liquid. It was Chanel No 5.

'She must have sat here,' she told Sarge.

Either side of the seated area were doors on two large cupboards.

Sarge stepped forward and pulled one open, partway at first, then fully when he saw what was there...

He let out a gasp.

Ellie spun round.

He opened the second door wide, shaking his head. When he spoke, his voice was barely audible. 'Look at this.'

Stuck on the inside of both doors were dozens of pictures, and newspaper clippings, of Sylvia: with Leonard, at the church; with the bell ringers; with the Bakery Book Club; at a village fête with Ellie and Zoe.

'This is some sort of shrine,' said Ellie, the hairs standing up on the back of her neck. 'Penelope was obviously obsessed with *Sylvia*.'

'I've read about this sort of thing but never expected to see anything like it.' Sarge was rubbing his chin and frowning.

Ellie photographed the two displays and slid her phone back in her pocket. 'We'll need to check the police have seen this – and inform Sylvia.'

'Definitely.' Sarge made sure Ellie was looking at him. 'Because if Penelope *didn't* do this, whoever *did* is dangerous.'

Downstairs, Zane wasn't about, so they left Mistletoe Manor straightaway and headed for the high street.

Sarge wanted to go home so Ellie thanked him for his help, said goodbye, and parked at the windmill.

As she let herself in, the jaunty sound of carols hit her ears. She wasn't looking forward to telling Sylvia about Penelope's shrine. The poor woman had just spent eleven hours in custody at the police station. There was, of course, a chance the police had already told her.

Rebus hurled himself at Ellie as the door opened.

She crouched down and gave him a hug.

'Greg nipped him over to the green for a leg stretch,' Sylvia shouted from the kitchen. 'How'd you get on at the manor?' She was still in her nightie, dressing gown and slippers.

'I've got something to tell you, I'm afraid,' said Ellie.

'Oh?' Her face drained of colour. 'That sounds ominous.'

Ellie kicked off her boots, hung up her coat and joined Sylvia at the kitchen table, sitting down next to her. 'We were in one of the guest rooms at Mistletoe Manor, looking for clues, and we stumbled on something very strange.' She relayed what they'd seen: the photos and newspaper clippings inside the dressing table cabinet.

Sylvia clamped her hand over her mouth.

'I take it the police didn't inform you?'

Sylvia shook her head. She was trembling. 'They might not have seen them. The crime scene was downstairs. If they were sure the crime started and ended down there, they wouldn't have searched the guest bedrooms, just her bedroom.'

'That makes sense,' said Ellie. 'It wasn't as if they needed to hunt for a murder weapon. Do you want to see some of the pictures?'

Sylvia nodded.

Ellie swiped her phone and passed it to Sylvia, who looked through the images in silence.

After a few minutes, she spoke. 'When I was a social worker, I knew a couple of cases where someone had done something similar to this,' Sylvia told Ellie. 'On both occasions, it was a symptom of some kind of fixation.' She paused. 'When Zoe asked if the catering arrangements had come about naturally, I thought she was being ridiculous.' Her voice trembled. 'Now, I'm not so sure.'

'Sorry.' Ellie put an arm round her. 'I know it's upsetting. Perhaps, in her head, it was a way of getting close to you; of finding out about you.'

But Sylvia's face was resolute. 'I want to see for myself. If Penelope made a shrine to me, I want to see it. I want to know why – and what she was up to.'

Chapter 29

While Sylvia had a relaxing bath and got dressed, Ellie nipped into the high street. As it was the week before Christmas, normal trading hours were relaxed and a lot of the shops were open longer, including today, a Sunday.

It was a long-standing matter of appreciation in Lower Wootton that the delicious aromas from Kathy's bakery reached your nose well before the shop came into view. This morning, Ellie smelled warm bread, chicken soup, fruity pies and sweet pastries.

'Any news about Sylvia?' Kathy asked anxiously as soon as she spotted Ellie.

Ellie beamed at her. 'They released her last night. The police can't keep you longer than twenty-four hours without applying for an extension or charging you.'

Kathy's eyebrows rose.

'Reading between the lines, I don't think there was any new evidence, so they had to let her go.'

'Very glad to hear it.' Kathy changed tack. 'Sorry to ask...'

Ellie wondered what she was going to say.

'I know it's not what's important, but people won't stop enquiring when her mince pies will be back in stock. They want to know if they can reserve some and if she'll be making her Christmas trifle too.'

Ellie chuckled. It was nice to know that Sylvia's baking was appreciated and her output in demand. 'Thanks, Kathy. I'll let her know... Is your hubby about? I wanted to pick his brains on council matters.'

Kathy's husband was the village handyman and a local councillor.

'He's helping Gladys Blackman this morning.'

'That's very kind of him, given it's the weekend.'

'Her family don't arrive until Christmas Eve, and she wants to get all the decorations up and looking nice before then.'

'Of course. She puts on that lovely lawn display every year. Zoe makes me walk that way with Reeby on Christmas Day so we can see it.'

'I'm sure if you pop round, she won't mind you having a chat with him,' said Kathy.

'Will do, thanks.' Ellie knew Gladys. She'd been one of her loyal cleaning clients for years. 'While I'm here, can I get a *pain au chocolat* and a coffee?'

'No problem. Speaking of Christmas trees, by the way, do you know who's delivering them locally now? Felix Wyndham.'

Ellie smiled. Village gossip could be annoying, but it was also extremely helpful at times, and she knew Kathy was only trying to give her a tip-off.

'I did, actually. He delivered to one of my customers and she told me. I've already spoken to him.' She lowered her voice. She'd known Kathy since their school days and counted her as one of her closest friends in the village. 'Got to say, I'm not finding it easy to form an opinion of Felix. Leonard talks about him affectionately...'

'He's a vicar though, Ells. He's going to speak nicely about people.' Kathy emptied the espresso holder of coffee grounds and refilled it.

'I know, but Zane says his father was a violent man.'

'Hmm. That's people though, isn't it? D'you remember at school: a new kid joined our class in year six? You used to sit with him in art and said he was lovely and fun. I couldn't stand him. Thought he was cocky and a bully. Who was right? Was one of us making up how we found him?'

'That's a good point. It's something Sylvia often talks about. People *are* different with different people. But how can Felix be nice *and* violent?'

'Our eldest has been doing a life coaching certificate,' Kathy said. 'She's now permanently telling Ted and I what we're doing and why, and how we could do things differently.'

Ellie laughed. She could picture the scene: Kathy's daughter, trying out her newfound knowledge and skills on her long-suffering parents.

'She says we've all got different facets to our personalities,or something. And that sometimes it's about what we choose to *show* people, and sometimes it's about what they *elicit* from us.' She shrugged. 'Make of that what you will.'

'Wow,' replied Ellie. 'That's impressive. All the conversation I get from Zoe at the moment is animal feeding regimes, DEFRA regulations and "is there any bread?"'

Kathy chuckled.

'Seriously, though, I've heard Sylvia say something similar. I suppose what they mean is: it *is* possible for Felix to be violent with Penelope and not violent with other people.'

'It's an upsetting business,' said Kathy. 'That's for sure.' She enveloped Ellie in a hug. 'I keep meaning to ask you: how's it going with Dave?' She bagged up a *pain au chocolat* and fixed a lid on Ellie's coffee. 'Sal said you've been on a few dates.'

'We have, and they've been lovely.' Ellie smiled. Butterflies fluttered in her tummy at the mention of Dave's name. 'But I'm so busy with my B&B guests and Blix Blitz, and now Penelope's death, I keep having to cancel.'

'I'm sure he understands. With his job, he must be busy too. And get called out at the last minute.' She handed Ellie her takeaway. Kathy must've picked up on her friend's unease.

'A bit.' Ellie frowned. She wasn't sure why her life seemed so unpredictable at the moment. 'It's not the same though. He's either on duty – or off. Whereas I seem to be always on call. If a guest locks themselves out, or' – she thought of her current guests – 'wants extra sugar, I have to be there.' Ellie told her about the fuse board the night before and the mouse on Bridget's bed.

'A kettle *and* hair straighteners on the same socket?' She sniggered. 'That would test most circuits. You'll figure it out. The B&B stuff is still new.'

'I'm enjoying it though. So many interesting people. Fascinating hearing about their lives. It's giving me lots of ideas for things I want to try.'

They said goodbye and Ellie headed for Mrs Blackman's. She'd walk. It was so pretty in the snow, and it gave her the opportunity to take in a bit of the village's magic.

In the high street, people were bustling about, collecting shopping, dashing into shops, chatting with neighbours. Outside the butcher's, chalkboards leaned against the façade, tempting passers-by.

Turkey. Goose. Duck. Pheasant. Partridge. Venison. Sausages. Pigs-in-blanket. Pork stuffing.

Ham and glazed gammon.

Nick and Charlie had cleared the pavement outside the shop so customers wouldn't have to queue with snow under their feet. Ellie waved as she went by and made a mental note to pick up the family's meat order.

When she arrived at the cul-de-sac and Gladys' bungalow, Ted's black pickup truck was on the drive. On the snowy lawn, white fairy lights illuminated two model reindeer and a sledge. Ted was up a ladder, trailing more fairy lights along the outside of the fascia boards and hooking them in place on the nails.

'Doesn't that look pretty?' Ellie said.

Ted turned. 'Hey Ells. Kath said you were on your way. Hang on. I'll come down.' He looped a length of lights around a hook several times and rested the spare cord in the gutter.

For a brief moment, Ellie thought about Penelope's killer.

Ted stepped off the bottom rung. 'Ells? You OK?'

'Sorry.' She shook her head. 'Miles away.'

'Kath said you're looking into Penelope's death.'

'Yes. This might be a long shot, but it's been bugging me for a couple of days.'

'I gather I need my council hat on?'

'Please. Do you know anything about any plans for Beech Farm? Development, for example? It seems odd that a place that size is lying unused. Most people would either sell it or rent it out – like the Selbys and Mistletoe Manor.'

'As it goes, I do. Felix Wyndham wants to change it into a retreat centre for artists.'

'Really? I was only talking to him yesterday. He didn't mention anything about it. And I got the impression he was done with art.'

Ted shrugged. 'Perhaps he's keeping quiet because he's on parole? Or because it might not happen?'

'What d'you mean, might not happen?'

'Beech Farm is currently classified as what's called a "dwelling house". His plans count as a material change of use, meaning he has to apply for planning consent for those changes to be lawful.'

'Ah. I see.'

'It will still be residential in the same way that hotels are. But the use becomes commercial.'

'Has consent been granted?'

'Not yet but it's at early stages. There are a number of objections related to the property being a listed building.

And quite a few complaints from neighbours, and those with vested interests.'

'Oh? Anyone in particular?'

'Not really. As far as I can remember, all pretty reasonable too. However, there's also the matter of the Land Registry. The deeds are still being updated. It takes months. I understood they'd been changed from jointly-owned into his wife's name.'

'Yes, Felix told me they'd been changed,' Ellie replied, 'and the Land Registry website still shows the title as being updated. He said they were changed into *her* sole name the year he went to prison.'

'Sounds about right,' Ted replied.

'How's he going to set the place up as a retreat centre when it doesn't belong to him?'

'This is part of the issue, I gather.'

'Ellie, dear,' came Gladys' friendly voice from the doorway. 'My cleaning day hasn't changed, has it?'

Ellie explained she wasn't here to work. 'Don't your decorations look terrific?'

They chatted for a few moments and Gladys went back inside to get warm.

Ellie reverted to the conversation with Ted. 'We were talking about the ownership of Beech Farm...'

'This is something the council is looking into. It'll affect his application if the planned development can't go ahead. And it can't if Felix doesn't own the property.'

'That makes sense, but his application doesn't. Does he not realise that?'

Ted shrugged. 'He's told a few people, not just you, that Zane is Penelope's heir. You might want to check that because...' he tapped his nose and winked, '... a little birdie told me otherwise.'

'Oh? Well, well.' Ellie's hand rose to her mouth as a thought occurred to her which changed everything. 'Hold up. The penny didn't drop on this when I first spoke to Zane.'

Ted stared at her expectantly.

'Given the deeds to Beech Farm were changed into Penelope's name when Felix went to prison, why are they still being updated? You said it took a few months.'

Ted nodded.

'Felix went to prison ten years ago. They can't still be responding to that modification.' She met Ted's gaze. 'Someone must've changed them again more recently.'

Chapter 30

When Ellie got back from talking to Kathy's husband, Sylvia said she hadn't seen much of Greg after their card game and suggested he'd spent the morning in the outhouse. Ellie wanted to check he was OK, to see if he wanted to join them for supper… *and* ask him a few more questions.

She and Sylvia crunched down the snowy path in the back garden.

James Stewart's voice made its way into Ellie's ears…

'You've been given a great gift, George…'

She gasped.

'… a chance to see what the world would be like without you.'

He was watching one of her favourite films: *It's a Wonderful Life.*

She knocked on the door, unable to stop herself from peering in. On the sofa, with Rebus in between them, were Sarge and Greg, each tucking into a giant bag of Maltesers and both captivated by the black and white film that was showing on Dave's large TV screen. Now she knew why, when Sarge had come back with her, he'd shot off so quickly.

Ellie pushed the door open a little further. 'Hello?'

'Oh, hi,' said Greg.

In fresh clothes, he was less dishevelled, and his greying hair looked almost distinguished.

'Come in. Is everything OK?'

'Hope you don't mind, I wanted to ask you a couple of questions about Mistletoe Manor.'

'Right. Sure.' He got up. 'Let me pause this so I can concentrate.'

'D'you want me to go?' Sarge asked her.

'It's up to your mate,' Ellie replied.

'You're alright.' Greg mock-punched his friend, as though they were teenagers still. 'No secrets from you.'

Rebus didn't stir, clearly in his element watching matinée films with his new buddies. Ellie hoped he hadn't scrounged any Maltesers.

She perched on the edge of the TV cabinet and Sylvia squeezed onto the sofa, making the others budge up.

'You're the person who spent the most time with Penelope Wyndham before her death,' said Ellie.

'Yes.'

'Who visited her? Anyone? I've somehow formed the impression she didn't have many friends, and wanted to check whether that's true or I've simply made it up.'

'Well, now. Let me think. You're right though: she didn't have many visitors. Some official in a suit and tie, and her son.'

Sylvia spoke now. 'Did Zane come on his own or with his wife and children?'

'On his own.'

'Who else?'

'Felix came to see her once.'

'Oh? He told me he last saw her at his sentencing.'

'Well, that's not true, I'm afraid. He definitely came to the house. I let him in; made them tea and a sandwich.'

'Goodness. That all sounds very cordial. I thought they weren't on good terms. In fact, no, I didn't just think it. Both Zane *and* Felix told me Felix and Penelope had an acrimonious relationship.'

Greg shrugged.

'How did things seem between them? Was it a tense encounter?'

'Things got a bit heated at one point. They talked, drank their tea, ate their sandwich, talked a bit more and then he left.'

'Do you know what they were discussing?' asked Sylvia.

'Not really. They kept their voices low. All I heard was something about her will.'

'Hmm. Anyone else visit?' Ellie didn't want to put names in his mouth, but she was interested to know if Toby Drysdale or Becky had been over to see her.

He shook his head. 'That's it.'

'What's the younger Mrs Wyndham like?' She was curious about Zane's wife.

'Never met her. Penelope said her daughter-in-law homeschools the children so she's pretty busy.'

'Any conflict when Zane was there?'

He frowned. 'Not that I heard, but I was clearing the snow from the step outside the kitchen door.'

Ellie, Sylvia and Sarge held each other's gaze, wondering what this news might mean.

Eventually, Sylvia spoke. 'I've just realised where I remember Zane's name from.'

Sarge stroked Rebus. 'Where?'

'Ells, d'you remember Zane mentioned he'd looked after his Mum when she was ill? I didn't doubt what he was saying. It had to go through Social Services as someone wanted him to become her official carer. If I remember correctly, I can check, he was made her Power of Attorney.'

'Were there questions then about her mental capacity?' Ellie asked.

'I don't know if it was that or he was simply being cautious. Penelope had a brain infection for quite some time and the doctors weren't sure if she was going to recover. It had affected her balance, her memory, her ability to process information, her coordination. It was awful. She was in a wheelchair for a while.'

'Wow,' said Sarge. 'That's serious and scary. I know that only too well. After my fall, I had surgery almost immediately and there wasn't any time to put plans in place. The circus had been my family for several years.'

'What did you do?' Sylvia asked him gently.

'Things were very different back then from how they are now. I had a district nurse come in and help me three times a day. I was in a wheelchair for nearly six months. Had intensive physiotherapy and hydrotherapy. Didn't know if I was ever going to walk again.'

Sylvia gave him a kind smile. 'I'm so glad you did.'

'I suppose what I mean is that it's quite something to give up two years of your life to be someone's carer,' said Sarge. 'I know Felix was in prison, but Zane must have loved his mother very much.'

As Ellie took in Sarge's words, her imagination was going crazy. What on earth had been going on?

Chapter 31

In the car on the way to Mistletoe Manor, Ellie, Sylvia and Sarge discussed the information Ted had given them about Felix and the ownership of Beech Farm.

'We need another chat with Felix, don't we?' said Ellie. 'First though, let's see what his son has to say about it all. If they've discussed it, that is.'

Ellie's phone rang.

'Hi, Ells.' It was Ted.

She put the call on loudspeaker.

'I've just remembered: there was a rather strange objection to the planning application for Beech Farm...'

'Oh?'

'Yeah. Lad around Zoe's age – maybe a bit older – stood up at a council meeting and said he had legal proceedings underway against Penelope and he didn't want anything to jeopardise the settlement he might get.'

'Was his name Toby Drysdale?' Sylvia shouted from the seat behind Sarge.

'That's him,' Ted replied. 'Seemed very upset about whatever it was that he claimed had gone on...'

Sylvia told Ted about Penelope allegedly stealing Toby's work.

'Oh, I heard about that,' came Ted's response. 'Is that who it was? Wow.'

'Pretty much what *we* said,' muttered Sarge.

'When was this meeting?' asked Ellie.

'Around two years ago.'

'So, the planning application's been going on for a while then?'

'Oh, they can take years, believe me. Especially when there are disputes about ownership.'

'Thanks, Ted. Keep us posted if you think of anything else, OK?'

'Will do. Kath and I will see you at the Christmas Fair on Monday. Bye.'

Zane met them on the steps of Mistletoe Manor, his long dreadlocks tied back and his face unshaven and creased.

Sylvia didn't bother with niceties. 'Ellie told me about the pictures your mother has of me.'

His cheeks went pink. 'The police mentioned them to me earlier. I'm… I'm… shocked.' He glanced about, seemingly perplexed.

'That makes two of us,' said Sylvia. 'If it's OK with you, I'd like to see them.' She'd been thinking about it ever since Ellie told her.

'Sure. I'll take you up.'

'That's OK,' Sylvia replied quickly. 'I know where the rooms are.' She didn't want someone staring at her, hurrying her along when she was trying to think and process what she was seeing. She threw a tiny smile in his direction.

'No problem.'

Sylvia, Ellie and Sarge traipsed into the hall and up the stairs, crossed the landing and went into the guest room. Both doors were open on the dressing table cabinet.

'Blimey. That's a lot of pictures.' Sylvia walked towards them, her pace slowing as she approached. 'I see what you mean.'

She'd done some reading up; confirmed that people who collated these sorts of images tended to be fixated on the person shown. What she wanted to establish was the defining feature. They usually clustered around a theme and that gave an indication of the type of fixation.

She tried to switch into her social worker mode. To scrutinise the images with the eyes of a professional, imagining the person shown wasn't her, but someone else. The target with her mother; with her granddaughter and grandson; with her adult children; laughing with her book club friends; at a committee meeting; judging a cake competition at a fair; bell ringing with locals.

Sylvia took out her phone and set about systematically taking snaps, reading the text that Penelope had cut out *and* the words she'd written in a marker. She analysed the images and the choice of settings and context.

After about ten minutes she turned to Ellie and Sarge, her face white as a sheet. 'I think I've figured it out. Everything she's pinned up revolves around a common theme.'

Ellie frowned. 'And?'

Chapter 32

Sylvia stood by the Aga in the kitchen at Mistletoe Manor and sipped the sweet tea that Zane had made for her. Ellie was pacing up and down while Sarge perched on a wooden chair.

'If you look carefully,' Sylvia told them, 'the images all refer to where I go, on what days, and who I'm with.'

Ellie had her phone out and was scrolling through her photographs. 'I agree. Penelope was interested in your routine; the people you mix with; your inner circle.'

'Yes. What these people do sometimes is try to insert themselves into the life of the person they're obsessed with, or into the lives of their friends and family.'

'That's so creepy. I wonder what she had planned.' Ellie was relieved Sylvia was safe. 'Did you know your mother had these images?' she asked Zane, who was staring out of the window. 'Did she talk to you about Sylvia?'

Before the three of them had come downstairs, they'd discussed how much to tell Zane, knowing he would likely be protective of his mother.

'No... and no.' He turned and faced them. 'I'm as stunned as you are. I mean, I knew Sylvia's late husband had put Dad away, but I had no idea Mum harboured bad feelings towards *her*. What can I say? I'm really sorry. I certainly don't share those feelings.'

'You didn't ever see her cutting out articles and images?' asked Sylvia.

He shook his head.

Perhaps it had been something Penelope kept hidden. Even from her son – the main person she had a relationship with.

'Is it possible Penelope was jealous of you?' Ellie asked Sylvia. 'Look. In every image, you're surrounded by people who love and respect you.'

Sylvia shrugged. 'It's possible, I suppose.'

Once Sylvia's colour had come back, and she'd finished her tea, she put her mug in the sink and said, 'While we're here, I'd like to have a look in the Great Hall, if that's OK.

I haven't been here since... since I found Penelope, and I'd like to see if anything comes to me while I'm back on the spot.'

She wanted to say she was convinced the clues to what happened to Penelope were in that room, but it sounded silly and she was tired.

'Of course,' Zane replied. 'I'll leave you to it.'

'Thanks.'

From the kitchen, Sylvia led them into the hall and then into the vast reception room where Penelope had been killed. As she stood in the doorway, shivers crept over her. Last time she was here, Penelope had been lying on the floor, dead. Her life extinguished. And no-one knew if her killer had still been in the house.

But it was more than that.

It was like stepping back in time.

On the previous occasion, Sylvia had been in a rush to find Penelope, so she hadn't been looking at windows and ceilings. Now she saw how ornate the room was, and the impression fell like a weight on her. There was something about the room that was deeply unsettling.

The ceiling was like a church's, arched, decorated and similar in height. She got wafts of wood and wax polish, and ash from the fire. Dark wooden panels ran up all the walls to head height. A stone mantelpiece lay over a giant inglenook fireplace. On it was a burst of gold tinsel and sparkly, silver baubles. Either side of the fire were two sets of floor-to-ceiling windows, set into the bays.

On the ceiling, a network of timber beams was set into the plaster. At one end of the room, a grandfather clock was beating out the seconds. Deer heads hung on the walls. The Selby family coat of arms, accompanied by swords. The Selbys were clearly a traditional family who liked hunting and the country life.

In one corner of the room, a black Steinway piano loomed majestically, as though it was waiting for someone to sit down and start playing to an audience. A mahogany dining table ran a quarter of the length of the room. Sylvia counted roughly forty high-backed, hand-carved, wooden chairs.

Why had Penelope wanted to live somewhere so grand, and with so much space? Sylvia thought of the intimate meals the Blixes had at the windmill, either around the table in the kitchen or on their laps in the lounge. Chatting while they ate. Surely Penelope hadn't sat in one of these wooden chairs on her own to eat her supper every evening?

And who was dusting all these cornices and waxing the wood?

At the opposite end of the room from the piano, the Christmas tree took pride of place again. It had lost a lot of decorations, and all of its fairy lights, but was at least vertical. The *chaise longue* was upright again.

'You OK?' Ellie put her hand on Sylvia's arm.

Sylvia nodded. 'It's just... weird being back here.' She shuffled over to the wall and turned, putting her back to the wooden panel. 'Was Penelope's killer still here when I arrived?' The same thought kept returning.

'Best not to dwell on that,' said Sarge.

'I agree,' said Ellie.

Sylvia wasn't going to be deterred. 'For her killer to strangle her with fairy lights; doesn't that suggest it *wasn't* premeditated? That whoever they were, they suddenly became overcome with a murderous rage...?' She walked over to the tree. 'They must've snatched up something that was close by that might serve as a murder weapon.'

'I think so,' Ellie replied, 'otherwise they'd have brought a rope or a knife or something with them, surely?'

Sylvia was nodding, deep in thought, striding this way and that as she sifted through ideas. 'I don't think, though, the use of fairy lights means it was *completely* spontaneous.'

'What d'you mean?' asked Ellie.

'I don't think they were some random person, who came in off the street on a whim and attacked her.'

'I'm sure the police will have considered whether this was a robbery that went wrong.' Sarge glanced about. 'I don't want to be rude but what is there to steal in a place like this? Dowdy antique furniture which weighs a ton? Stuffed deer heads which are probably full of fleas? And who would want someone else's family coats of arms?' He shook his head. 'No, this wasn't a burglary.'

'When I was a social worker, I had a client whose mother killed her father,' Sylvia told them. 'It was an abusive situation which had gone on for years. Every day the pressure increased, and so did the toll it took on the family. Until one day, the mother snapped. One final humiliation released all the years of suppressed rage.' Sylvia stared at Ellie and Sarge in turn. 'I think this is what we're dealing with. Whoever came here and killed Penelope had been contemplating it for a while. Something happened either on Thursday, or while they were here, which was the final straw for them.'

'Makes sense,' Ellie replied.

'The main question is, who was it? Who was sufficiently full of hate towards her to want her dead?' The question sent a chill over Sylvia. 'And what happened to trigger the fatal act?'

'It might be that we find out about the event or events,' said Ellie, 'and that leads us to the killer. We've got to keep digging.'

Sarge had wandered over to one of the bay windows. 'Changing the subject, if I may... I would like to know how her killer got in. Were they already in the house when Penelope got back from switching on the lights? Were they lying in wait for her?'

Ellie remembered what Zoe had told them from the event in the village. 'Don't forget, Penelope told Zoe she was being followed and she was anxious to get back here.'

Sylvia drew in a deep breath. 'When we asked Greg what happened when they arrived back, he said Penelope had resurrected her accusations. The impression I got was that as soon as that happened, he went upstairs, packed up his belongings and left.'

'That's exactly what he did,' said Sarge. 'He told me he left immediately after that. Before she got the chance to say anything else.'

'Are we certain Greg told us the truth?' said Sylvia.

'Of course.' Sarge let out a loud tut.

Sylvia knew the police would take samples from Greg. Find out if he was involved. 'Sorry,' she told Sarge. 'We know he's your friend, but we have to ask questions and make sure we're thorough.'

Sarge continued to look out of the window, then stepped back and changed perspective, as though he was making mental calculations.

'In houses like these, the Grand Hall often runs along the front of the house,' he informed them, 'and parts of the room are visible from the drive. Similarly, people can often see *out* from the hall as well.' He settled in one position. 'For example, from here, I can see who's coming through the gates.' He shifted a little. 'From *here* I can see who's at the front door.' He paced towards the other end of the room. 'From *here*, I can see out over the gardens and the lake.'

'What are you suggesting?' Sylvia asked him, a lilt of excitement creeping into her voice. 'That Penelope might've seen her killer arriving?'

'Well, yes, possibly. I'm not completely sure what I'm suggesting. There's something scratching at the edges of my brain about Penelope being killed in here. Did she know her killer? Did they let themselves in with a key and found her here? Or did she let them in via one of the doors and bring them in here?'

'Good questions,' Sylvia replied. 'My sense is that – for the killer to be in here with her – it had to be someone she knew. Otherwise, she'd have talked to them in the hall or at the door, surely, and been killed there?'

Sarge had got Sylvia thinking. She was preoccupied with where an attacker may have come from. 'Supposing the killer was here when Penelope got home. There are plenty of places for them to have lain in wait.' She spun round, gesturing. 'Behind the Christmas tree... crouched down behind the piano... under the table... behind one of the many curtains.' She pointed over at the long length of peacock-green velvet which hung on poles over each window.

'Hiding makes sense,' said Ellie, shuddering. 'It would be pretty alarming for someone to leap out at you from behind one of those curtains.'

'Are you telling me that, in her terrified state, she then thought to pick up her notepad and write the number '7' on it?'

Sarge's sarcasm earned him a dirty look from Sylvia. 'When you put it like that, no. It sounds preposterous. But what if she saw the killer arrive while she was writing her shopping list? They were shouting, and scared her enough for her to fear for her life and she wrote–'

'... the number seven? Why?'

Sylvia let out a groan. 'I don't know,' she snapped. 'It sounds ridiculous now. The number probably has nothing to do with her death.'

'OK, let's start again,' said Ellie.

'Let's think about the timing,' said Sylvia. 'I arrived here around an hour before the reception, and she was already dead.'

'Shall we discuss how they made their exit,' said Sarge. 'It's likely the killer will have been keen to be careful. They won't have wanted anyone seeing them, assuming they knew that guests were going to be arriving imminently.'

'They could have gone into the hall and out of the front door, although that seems the least likely.' Sylvia inched forward to cast her gaze over the drive. 'From there, unless they went round the side of the house, the only exit route was down the drive, risking discovery.' She turned to the side wall. 'They could have left through the back door and across the fields?'

'I know where those fields lead to,' said Ellie. 'Reeby and I have walked along there. They bring you out on the old railway line round the back of Coldblow Crossing.'

'Ah.' Sylvia's gaze fell on the hardwood floor.

Sarge was standing at the window at the opposite end of the room from the piano. Despite the earlier snowfall, the sun had now come out and a thick shard of light fell across the parquet.

'Look.' Sylvia pointed. 'I can see powdery footprints. They look like when Rebus has been in the snow and has brought salt in on his pads. And it's dried.'

Sylvia squatted down on the ground and Ellie joined her.

'Those are unusual marks,' said Ellie. 'That's not a welly boot or a trainer.'

Ellie snapped a couple of photos of the footprint on her phone. She placed her hand flat, next to one of the prints, taking care not to touch any of them or the floor, presumably to give an idea of scale and size.

'I've seen those markings somewhere,' said Sylvia. 'Now I just need to remember where.'

Chapter 33

Felix groaned when he caught sight of Ellie and Sylvia. His gaze darted nervously from one side of the yard to the other. 'I had a feeling you'd be back.' This time he plunged his axe into a log and left it there. Brushed dirt off his hands and turned to speak to them.

'I bet you did,' Sylvia replied. 'Seems you told us several porkies.'

He cleared his throat.

Ellie and Sylvia had discussed what to ask him.

'Shall we start with the tea and sandwich you had with your wife a couple of weeks ago?' Sylvia asked, while Ellie observed.

'Ah. Hargrave.'

'You said you hadn't seen your wife since your sentencing hearing.'

'We had things to discuss.'

'I don't doubt it. But why lie and say you hadn't seen her?'

'I don't have to explain my life to you.' He started moving nets of logs from one side of the barn to the other. 'That's the ash.' He counted the nets. 'Oak. Two, four...'

'True. I gather you were discussing a retreat centre. Would that have been the one you're wanting to convert Beech Farm into?'

'Don't know what you're talking about. Two. Four. Six. Eight. That's the silver birch.'

'Oh, come on. The planning application?'

He shrugged.

'OK, let's try this question,' said Ellie. 'You were in one of my photos at the switching-on of the lights. With a blonde woman. Yet you said you weren't there. Why?'

'I said I was working that evening. I was.'

Ellie showed him the photo. 'Is this woman your new girlfriend?'

He grunted. 'Something like that. Sweet chestnut: two, four. We were there for about twenty minutes. Six, eight. Her kids wanted to see the lights. I went back to my deliveries afterwards.'

'Have you given her name to the police?'

'Not yet.'

'But she'll confirm she was with you, will she?'

'We'll soon find out, won't we?'

'Whose was the next delivery you did and what time was it?'

'Big old manor house on Church Lane, just along from St Mary the Virgin in Ripple. Wrought iron gates, fountain. Got to them just after 6pm.'

'I know the one. Ripple House.'

Ellie signalled for Sylvia to take over.

'Did you know about the shrine your wife had to me in her guest room?'

'The what? No.' He began stacking kindling.

'You sure?' asked Sylvia.

'Of course I'm sure. Why would she have a shrine to you? If anyone should have a beef with you, wouldn't it be *me*? *I* was the one your husband put in prison.'

'Someone told the police they saw me murdering her. I've just spent eleven hours in custody under arrest.'

Ellie and Sarge stepped forward, standing either side of Sylvia.

'And you think that was me?' Felix's eyes were blazing.

'I don't know who it was. But it seems like someone has a grudge against me.'

'Well, you can believe what you like but I don't. I don't even particularly have issues with your late husband. I was guilty. But – I served my time. And I did *not* try to frame you with the police.'

'There's another possible explanation.' Sarge had his hands in his pockets. 'Oldest trick in the book. The person who told the police they saw you strangle Penelope didn't do it for revenge. They did it to divert attention away from them. In other words, it was the killer.'

'Makes sense,' said Ellie. 'Can we ask you some financial questions now, please?'

'If you must.'

'Presumably you've been in contact with the executor of your wife's will. Who is her beneficiary?'

'As far as I know, it's Zane. But one of the reasons why Penelope and I met was because she'd decided she'd made a mistake, cutting me out of everything, and wanted to change her will.'

'Oh?'

'To include me.'

'Did she say what had brought about the change of heart?' asked Sarge.

'No.'

'She must have. Didn't you ask?'

He snorted. 'Look at me. This is my life now. OK, it's nobody's fault but my own but I've had to start from scratch. Half the time, I'm so tired, I crash out here in a sleeping bag and can't be bothered to drag myself back to my room at the pub. Do you think, if my wife was going to give me a leg-up financially, I'm going to say no? Or ask her why?'

'Why was she doing a will?' asked Sarge. 'Did you both make them?'

'When she had meningitis, she was advised to do it. Zane helped her.'

'OK,' said Ellie. 'Sticking with finances, did your wife own a yacht?'

Felix nodded. 'Yes. Apparently, Zane bought it for her. At least, that's what she told me.' He paused. 'Gotta hand it to my son. Those wellness products aren't my cup of tea, but he's made a fortune from them.'

'Online it says your son developed the range while he was looking after your mother. Is that correct?'

'If that's what it says.'

It was a typical Felix answer.

'It was pretty kind of him to go over to the US with her and look after her.'

Felix raised his eyebrows. 'Well, I was banged up.'

'I had life-changing back surgery many years ago,' said Sarge. 'Believe me, I know how rare it is that someone will put their life on hold like that to look after you.'

'Is that right?'

'Mr Wyndham,' Ellie said gently, 'we know you and your son don't... er... have the easiest relationship. You've got to admit he's been a good son to her, though, no?'

'If you say so.' His words were clipped. He paused, as though he was debating whether to add something. 'There is one thing I'll tell you...'

'What's that?' asked Sylvia.

'That young writer whose work my wife stole...'

'Toby?'

'That's him.'

'What about him?' Ellie was curious about Felix's word choice. If he'd thought Toby had been in the wrong, wouldn't he have said something like, '... who made crazy allegations...'

'Nice lad.'

Ellie wondered what was coming.

'I felt very sorry for him. Another fly in my wife's trap. But – there was something strange going on with him.'

'What d'you mean?'

'He's been hanging about recently.'

Chapter 34

The children's carol service at St Mary's was one of Ellie's favourite things to do at Christmas. The pretty church was resplendent with flower arrangements, wreaths and candles. The stained-glass windows shone in the evening light. The giant fir tree stood proudly in the stone arch, a mass of golden stars and twinkling lights.

Around the crib, local children of all ages had assembled, and the nativity story had just ended.

Ellie, Zoe and Sylvia were standing for the last carol.

'Once in Royal David's city,' sang the choir and congregation, *'stood a lowly cattle shed.'*

The three of them belted out the words they'd known since they were children.

'Where a mother laid her baby...'

Kathy from the baker's was dressed up as Mary, and her husband was Joseph.

'In a manger for his bed.'

'Love Ted's wig,' Zoe whispered to Ellie. 'No wonder Dad sticks to Father Christmas.'

'Mary was that mother mild...'

When the carol finished, Leonard concluded the service. 'Thank you all for gathering today to share the nativity story and the birth of Jesus.' He smiled round at the congregation. 'Just as Mary and Joseph made their journey to Bethlehem, you've made your way here. We've had shepherds, kings, sheep, donkeys and angels. We pray for peace in all the world. May the joy of the angels be with you this Christmas and always.'

The choir filed out, cassocks and surplices flowing. People began to leave their pews, and the church staff cleared away service sheets.

The Blixes made their way over to Toby, who was sitting four rows from the front. Zoe had popped round to his house and his mum had said he was going to the service.

'Hey, Toby,' said Ellie. 'Better than Pink Floyd, eh?'

'Mrs Blix,' he said. He flickered a polite smile at Zoe and Sylvia and pulled his beanie further down over his forehead.

Sylvia stood back so as not to crowd him out.

'We're really sorry about what happened with Penelope Wyndham,' Ellie continued. 'We understand how angry you must be.'

He nodded.

'We've heard about the planning meeting. We've also heard you've been hanging around Penelope recently.'

He didn't speak.

'Did you exaggerate the agoraphobia?'

He shook his head, lips clenched together like he was holding onto tears. 'No. I've recently started some new medication which is helping.'

'Did you go over to Mistletoe Manor the night Penelope was killed?'

He let out a sob. Glanced about the church anxiously. 'Yes.'

'Toby, this is very serious. Have you told the police this?'

'No. I was worried they'd think I murdered her.'

'Did you talk to her?' Thoughts were racing through Ellie's head.

He shook his head again, his hands over his mouth.

'Was she alive when you got there?'

'I don't think so.'

'Did you see anyone while you were there?'

'No. But I heard someone. They were leaning over her body. I was scared, so I ran.'

'Were they male or female?'

'A woman. She had long hair.'

Chapter 35

While Ellie was in the bath, Sylvia sat cross-legged on the carpet in the lounge, next to the Christmas tree. Out in front of her were all the things she'd gathered from the case. Article printouts, photographs, pages of her notes, her list of the main characters and their inter-relationships.

Penelope.

Felix.

Becky.

Toby.

Greg.

Zane.

Sally's mother, Felicity.

Rebus lay behind her, on his side, his warm back against hers, his paws stretched out in the other direction, twitching as he dreamt.

She'd switched off the carols. She needed silence to allow her thoughts to converge, determined to figure out who killed Penelope.

Piece by piece, she reviewed everything they'd learnt since Thursday. Penelope's greed. Felix's collusion. Becky's disappointment and hurt. Toby's sense of betrayal. Felicity's shock at learning Becky was her daughter. Greg's row with Penelope. Zane's dedication to his mother.

Sylvia studied their faces in the images. Penelope's brittle elegance. Felix's scruffy warmth. The kindness of Sally's mum. Toby's pained intelligence. Becky's searing honesty. Zane's compassion. Greg's loyalty.

One person connected them all: Penelope Wyndham.

Sylvia remembered bumping into Penelope in the bakery a few weeks earlier. The event which had started all this. Where Penelope had put on her performance and asked Sylvia to do her catering. She hadn't consciously realised at the time that she'd felt manoeuvred. She'd felt flattered and curious.

She was relieved to have spoken to Dave about the shrine. Hopefully – although it wasn't what she would have wanted – with Penelope dead now, any plans she had to cause trouble for Sylvia had died with the woman.

She thought about Felix. He seemed to arouse different reactions in people. The lovable rogue and the violent man. Was his alibi to be trusted, or was she lying to protect her man? When Penelope had suggested the art fraud, had he felt flattered and needed? Important?

Sylvia had met toxic individuals like Penelope before. When they imposed their will, people bent to accommodate them; anxious to please, to be graced with their attention.

She then considered Greg, leaving the manor house where he'd worked for decades on the very evening Penelope was killed. Sarge had been finding it hard to see his schoolfriend as a killer, but several things didn't quite add up.

Next, her thoughts went to Toby and his brittleness and vulnerability. He was justifiably angry with Penelope for stealing his work and sabotaging his writing career. Would he ever get over the betrayal? Had he ruined his own life by killing her? She hoped not. His words at the church kept playing on a loop in her head. He'd seen a long-haired woman in the Great Hall, leaning over Penelope's body.

Then there was Becky and her painful feelings of rejection. Had these finally spilled over and pushed her to kill her stepmother? She undoubtedly had a deeply personal motive... and the rage.

Zane was also on her mind, with his enduring love for his mother, his wellness business. Meeting him in the barn where he was feeding the sheep in his townie clothes. She thought about the time he'd devoted to looking after his mother and to his business. The new range of drinks he was about to launch. He was the person she felt the most sorry for – along with Becky.

Felix had a motive. Penelope had set him up to carry out criminal acts to enable her to lead the sort of lifestyle she wanted, and he'd gone along with it. So, he was a people-pleaser and a coward. Did that make him a murderer? Zane had been at pains to depict his father in violent terms. Becky and the vicar hadn't conveyed the same impression.

Finally, there was Sally's mum. Could she have wanted Penelope dead?

Sylvia cast her gaze over the pictures in front of her. Something was bugging her about Becky. It was her Facebook background photo. A picture of her with her family, tobogganing on Hawksdown a few days earlier in the snow. Rosy-cheeked children, hair flying in the snowy breeze. The giant Parka which Ellie had seen Becky wearing. The cosy yellow boots.

The boots.

She pulled the photo towards her of the footwear marks from the Great Hall. The distinctive treads, made to look like real toes.

She reflected on what they knew about Felix. His relationship with Zane. What Zane had told them about his father. The wellness products. The planned retreat centre. The changes to Penelope's will. Greg's row with her. The disruption Becky's 'arrival' had caused.

As she visualised the events and characters in her mind, the last piece of the puzzle fell into place, and it all made sense. She finally knew who'd killed Penelope. And if they weren't quick – the person was likely to kill again.

'Ellie? Ells?' Sylvia shouted. 'I've figured it out. I know who did it. We need to hurry.' She clattered up the stairs and barged into the bathroom, excitedly filling Ellie in on what she'd deduced, and how.

'I suggest we meet at Mistletoe Manor,' said Ellie.

'I agree,' replied Sylvia. 'Can you call Dave? Ask him to meet us there at 9pm with Felix and Toby?'

Ellie was pulling on her jeans and jumper. 'Sure. Zoe's gone back to Finn's but we'll need her too. I'll ring her in a sec.' She tied her hair in a ponytail. 'Penelope and her family deserve justice,' she said. 'And we all need to feel safe in Wootton again.'

'Before we gather everyone, we need to speak to Sally's mum,' said Sylvia. 'Find out if she is Becky's mother. *And* have a word with Becky. Once we've done that, Becky can come with me to pick up Zane.'

'Shall I bring Sally and her mum, and Greg and Sarge?'

'Please,' said Sylvia. 'That's the logistics sorted. We're all set. Let's go.'

Chapter 36

At nine o'clock in the evening, the Great Hall at Mistletoe Manor felt imposing. Sylvia and Ellie had switched on a few lamps. The Christmas tree lights were off. This wasn't a time for celebration.

Chairs cordoned off the area where Sylvia had seen footprints.

Zane and Becky were standing as far apart as they could. Becky sat on a chunky radiator in one of the bay windows, nervously clutching her phone. Zane stood with his back to the fireplace, continually checking his watch. Greg and Sarge had come in Ellie's jeep. The two friends perched on a brown, leather Chesterfield sofa. Sally had followed them in her car with her mum. The two women stood with Felix and Toby, who'd arrived with Dave and Zoe.

Dave had made sure all the floor-to-ceiling windows were locked and was standing guard by the door.

Sylvia took a deep breath and began.

'What I didn't expect when we began this investigation was that I was going to be arrested for Penelope's murder. I don't yet know who's responsible for that but I'm confident it will emerge shortly. It didn't achieve much. OK, I was out of action for the eleven hours I spent in custody, and I would've much preferred to have spent that time tracking down Penelope's killer. However, it served to make me all the more determined.' She faced the group, her expression one of resolve.

Ellie took over.

'Each time we undertake an investigation in the village, it always assumes a distinct tone of its own. This one has been characterised by the amount of people we had to track down who had either gone AWOL, or who were choosing to live under the radar.'

Sylvia again.

'When someone is killed, just as the police do, we always start with the victim's life, family and work. There was a lot to get our teeth into with Penelope, as she had recently come out of retirement and resumed writing.

She had recovered, against the odds, from a very serious meningitis infection. She'd been on the receiving end of legal proceedings over allegations of stealing a student's work.' She nodded at Toby. 'And she'd had to cope with her husband being convicted of art fraud.'

Felix grunted.

'I think it's fair to say we've uncovered things which frankly we wish we hadn't, and, sadly, you probably will too.' Ellie fixed her gaze on the first person. 'Felix, let's start with you.'

He rolled his eyes, and the energy ratcheted up in the room. 'Here we go.'

'Your daughter,' Ellie gestured to Becky, 'told us that the art fraud you were convicted of was Penelope's idea, not yours. Is that correct?'

'It is.'

'And do you have evidence proving that?'

'I do.'

Dave's eyebrows rose.

'Was this evidence submitted as part of your criminal investigation?'

'Some of it was, yes. But I now have much more, thanks to Becky.'

'That's beyond the scope of this investigation,' said Ellie, 'but I'm sure the police will be more than happy to assess this new information.'

Dave nodded.

'However, what's important from our point of view is that this surely must have given you a reason to feel extremely angry with your wife. Is that fair?'

'Very fair. I've felt furious with her for years.'

'Enough to want her dead?'

'It's certainly something I fantasised about, if you like. Only in my head, of course. When I discovered all the ways in which she was deliberately trying to manipulate me, take advantage of me, use me and set me up to take the fall, all for her financial gain, I was very angry indeed.'

'Can someone account for your whereabouts on Thursday evening when Penelope was killed?'

'Yes. Several of my customers will be able to.' He repeated what he'd told Ellie about delivering Christmas trees and stopping off to watch the lights with his partner. 'She will be able to confirm this for you and the police. After that, I resumed my deliveries and finally clocked off at about 10.30pm.'

Sylvia took over. 'Can you explain to us why your son, Zane, describes you as being a violent man?'

'Possibly. But I'd only be guessing. It's best you ask him.'

'For example, he told us that you attempted to strangle your wife with fairy lights when he was growing up. Is this true? Yes or no, please.'

'No.'

'And that you were regularly threatening to kill her.'

'Also untrue. We had arguments, as all couples do. Nothing more.'

'So why did he say it?'

'You'll have to ask him.' He gestured to Zane, who tutted.

'Thank you. We will. Now, turning to your wife's finances, there are a number of conflicting situations we'd like to clear up. Firstly, who owns Beech Farm?'

'My wife, currently. When her estate is settled, it will be whoever her benefactor is.'

'And who is that?'

'She told me it's our son, Zane.'

'Isn't it true that you had been trying to convince your wife to change her will and to make you a beneficiary after all?'

'No, it isn't.' Anger flashed over his face. 'Where did you get that from?'

'Allow us to ask the questions, Mr Wyndham, please,' said Sylvia, in her best headmistressy voice.

He raised his hand in submission.

'Isn't it also true that you were annoyed about having to sign over ownership of Beech Farm to your wife, and furious that she had left you out of her will altogether?'

'Of course. How would you feel? Yes, it's true that I conducted the art fraud negotiations as I had the contacts, but, rightly or wrongly, Penelope benefited from those as much as I did. And, although I appreciate a lot of people might not believe me, the art fraud was *her* idea in the first place. So, it was pretty rich of her to basically take everything from me when I went to prison – and blame me.'

'Do continue.'

'However, as misguided as I obviously was, I am not so stupid as to make a second serious mistake. In other words, however difficult she was determined to make my life, I have started again from scratch in *legal*,' he emphasised the word, 'employment.'

'Thank you. Zane, let's come to you next.'

'Sure.' He stood up straight, reminding Sylvia of a swotty head boy at school.

'You adored your mother, didn't you?'

'Absolutely. She was a wonderful woman.'

'She must have been very appreciative of you looking after her when she was ill? And all the things you did to help her.'

Sylvia saw Sarge listening intently.

He shrugged, embarrassed. 'I just did what felt right.'

'Didn't you want to go to the switching on of the lights?'

'I did, but we discussed it as a family and made the decision not to go. My wife was tired, and we have a rule at home that if one of us is on empty, we rest up.' He smiled. 'It's one of the four pillars of well-being, according to Wyndham Wellness.'

'Of course. Sounds like a very good idea. What did you do instead?'

'We made some food, played carols and did a jigsaw, and had an early night.'

'That was all four of you, yes?'

'That's correct. We try, as much as possible, to do everything together as a family.'

'And how did that work when you were in the USA, looking after your mother?'

'My wife and I had only just started dating at that point. We took a break so I could accompany Mum overseas where she could get the treatment she needed. When I got back, we picked up our relationship, got married and had children.'

'Thank you. Becky, let's come to you now. Everyone who's read the *Wootton Gazette* will by now know that Felix is your biological father.'

Becky nodded, stuffing her phone in her pocket.

'You told us that Penelope hated you and you felt similar.'

'That's correct. She went out of her way to make it as difficult as possible for me to see my father.'

'You've told us how painful this has been for you. My question to you is: was this enough to make you want to get rid of Penelope?'

'It was certainly enough to make me think about it. A bit like Felix, I suppose I fantasised about it sometimes too. A life without the woman who was making that life difficult.' She threw her hands up as though it was a no brainer. 'However, many of us live with situations which are extremely onerous, stressful and unpleasant, and we don't murder the person responsible. I have a husband who I love very much. Children who are my world, and amazing adoptive parents. Do you really think I'm going to do something which would result in me going to prison for my whole life, depriving my husband of his wife and depriving my children of their mother?'

'Forgive me, but that is exactly the sort of answer a killer would give. Isn't it?'

A gasp went round the room.

'I mean, you're not exactly going to say, "Oh yes, it was me. I did it." Are you?'

'Of course not.'

'You see, a witness saw you in the Great Hall leaning over your stepmother's body, either just before or just after she was killed. How do you explain that?'

'It's impossible, because I wasn't there.' She surveyed the room, anxiously checking faces. 'Like most of us here, and most of us living in the area, I went with my family to see the lights being switched on in Wootton. I was keen *not* to bump into my stepmother, so we didn't stay very long, and we returned home to Martin Mill shortly after everything finished.'

'Can I ask you about your walking boots?'

Becky frowned. 'These?' She pointed to her feet.

'Yes. Would you mind taking one of them off so we can see the sole?'

'If you insist.' She bent over, untied and removed her boot and handed it to Ellie.

Zoe handed her mum a printout of the tread they'd found on the floor in the Great Hall.

'Would you agree that the sole of your boot has a very similar tread to the one in this photograph?'

'It looks very much like it, yes.'

'Where did you get your boots from?'

'From Zane's wellness website. I have trouble with plantar fasciitis. My husband had been having a nose at the website and saw that this boot is designed to help. He bought them for me as a birthday present.'

'Thank you. Before I move on, can you please confirm for us when you last made contact with your biological mother?'

'About five years ago.'

'Are you sure about that?'

'I don't remember the precise date, if that's what you're asking me, but I will be able to check when it was very easily. It'll be in my email.'

'And, just to be clear, you haven't been in touch again recently?'

'I have not.'

'Thank you.' Ellie turned to Sally's mother. She and Sally stood next to each other, arms clasped. 'Mrs. Jones?'

'Yes.'

'This is very odd for me as I've known you all my life.'

'It's very odd for me too.'

'You've confirmed you would like to share something with us. Is that correct?'

She nodded, glancing nervously over at Becky. 'Becky Wyndham is my biological daughter.'

Becky smiled and nodded.

'I, very sadly, had to have her adopted after getting pregnant when I was young.'

'We appreciate that this must be really difficult for you,' said Ellie. 'And I'm only asking you about it in case it's relevant to Penelope's murder.'

Another gasp went round the hall.

'Isn't it true that, when Becky got in touch with you through the Adoption Society, Penelope Wyndham put pressure on you to stay out of Becky's life?'

'Sadly, it is true. I very much regret this and wish I could turn back the clock and do things differently. She found out through Felix.'

'How did you feel about Penelope's behaviour?'

'I was incensed. I assumed, in my naivete, that it was because she wanted to have a relationship with Becky, so when I found out she didn't, and she didn't seem to want Becky to have a relationship with her father either, I was even more angry.'

She opened her mouth as if to say more, then stopped, then changed her mind back.

'Now, I'm going to be the third person to say that I, too, fantasised about a world without Penelope, where Becky could have had a relationship with me and with Felix. And I'm going to be the third person to say, no, I did not kill her.' She paused for breath. 'Like the others, I was also at the switching-on of the lights in the village, and I didn't hurry home afterwards as it was such a beautiful evening, and the atmosphere was wonderful. Everyone happy and excited. The only thing marring it for me was that I had to put up with seeing Penelope's smug face switching the lights on. Acting like she was an A-list celebrity.'

In her peripheral vision, Ellie caught sight of someone waving their arm. It was Toby.

'Please,' he said. 'I need to say something. That wasn't who I saw.' He pointed at Becky. 'I know I said it looked like her, but it wasn't *her*. The person I saw was much taller. More athletic.'

'I'm very pleased to hear you say that,' Sylvia told Toby, 'because I suspected it wasn't Becky either. Thank you. I was hoping for that confirmation.'

Toby let out a sigh of relief and patted his chest.

'I think that *you*, Mr Wyndham,' she looked straight at Zane, 'were in the Great Hall and it was you Toby saw.'

'I'm finding it hard to know whether you're joking or not,' Zane replied. 'I've told you. I was nowhere near Mistletoe Manor. I was at home with my family. You're going to need to go back to the drawing board.'

'I can assure you I am not joking about anything. We have a witness who overheard your mother talking to Felix about her will.'

'She wanted to change it,' shouted Felix, 'that's why. But no doubt Mr Control Freak Wellness here didn't want her to.' He dragged his hand through his hair, as though he was gathering his thoughts. 'And, as far as I know, she died before she could change it. Why was that then, Zane?'

Everyone stared at the two men.

Sylvia waited for a few moments, then said to Zane, 'You'll know all the ways in and out of Mistletoe Manor. I couldn't help noticing your boots the day we met you. You were feeding the sheep in their pen in your town clothes.' She pointed at his feet. 'They're the same shoes as Becky's.' She held up the printout of the treads from near where Penelope's body had lain.

'And?' said Zane sarcastically. 'Of course my shoe treads are in here. So, probably, will my DNA be. Because I've been here regularly visiting my mother.'

'That's not true, Mr Wyndham. Is it?'

It was Greg.

He stood up.

'I've only ever seen you at the manor house *once*,' Greg told them, his tone sombre. 'And on that occasion, you weren't in the Great Hall. You were in the kitchen because your mother was baking a sponge cake, and she asked me to bring you in. The fire wasn't made in here, and you stayed in the kitchen the whole time.'

'You weren't here every time I came,' Zane replied. 'In fact, one time Mum said you'd gone into the village for bread.'

'I doubt that very much because, after you'd gone, I commented on how nice it was that you'd visited. D'you know what she said?'

Everyone was watching him.

'She snorted and said, "Yes, the first and last time, I expect. He's not going to be happy with me when he finds out what I've done".'

'That could mean anything.' Zane forced a laugh. 'She might've been talking about what we were going to eat for Christmas dinner. She always... er... forgets we're vegetarians.'

'Except she wasn't talking about food. That afternoon, she asked me to take her to the solicitor's in the village.' He turned to Dave. 'I'm sure they'll be able to confirm what changes she'd made to her financial arrangements.'

'If I can add to that?' said Ellie. 'The Land Registry cannot still be updating from when Penelope changed the farmhouse deeds into her name. That was ten years ago. The police can verify this, but I suspect that Penelope made a much more recent change. I suspect it'll tie in with the changes she made to her will.'

Greg waited for her to finish and faced Zane again. 'Going back to the footprints, given I showed you into the kitchen and out of the front door the day you visited, it means your footprints are in here from the evening of your mother's death.'

Ellie paused to allow the news to sink in. 'Of course, the police will be able to compare the prints in a far more accurate and technical way than me holding up a piece of paper. But it's not looking good, is it? So far, we have means and opportunity.'

'This is complete nonsense,' Zane snapped. 'It's pure fantasy. I adored my mother. Why on earth would I kill her?'

'To stop her from changing her will and signing the farmhouse over to Felix.' Sylvia ploughed on. 'This was what clinched it for me. It was very clever of you to put the planning application for the retreat centre in your father's name so no-one would think it was you.'

Zane's face clouded over.

'Were you waiting until her estate was settled and were you then going to change it into your name?'

'No idea what you're talking about.'

'OK. Let's test that.' She turned away from him. 'Felix, did you put in a planning application to change the use of Beech Farm from a dwelling to a commercial retreat centre?'

'Absolutely not.'

She faced Zane again. 'How do you explain that?'

He shrugged.

'You needed ownership of the farm to fall to *you*, didn't you? And if your mother changed her will to include your father after all, that wasn't going to work, was it?'

'Wow,' said Felix. 'I've always known you're exactly like your mother: greedy, manipulative, ruthless...'

'Your mother wasn't writing an "L" on her notepad, was she? Or a "7".' Sylvia held up a piece of A4 paper on which she'd replicated Penelope's '7'. 'She was writing a "Z". You must've come in. She realised she was in danger and tried to quickly scribble your name.'

Zane blushed.

'But she dropped the pad and pen before she managed to complete it. I'm right, aren't I?'

He stared at her. Silent. Defiant.

Ellie took over. 'When I walk Rebus along the old railway line,' she told everyone, 'it brings me into a lane and a field which backs onto Mistletoe Manor. There's a CCTV camera on the corner there because it's a bit of a blind spot and there have been a few accidents. If the police check it at, say, 5.30pm, what are the chances of them finding you sneaking into your mother's posh rental home from the rear?'

Zane shrugged.

'I also suspect you told everyone your father is violent as it helped you to frame him as a suspect in your mother's murder. Did you persuade your mum to put the rental agreement for Mistletoe Manor in Becky's name, so as to conserve your inheritance?'

'Oh,' exclaimed Becky. 'We wondered why we got that bill. I simply sent it on to her with a rude message.'

Ellie continued. 'Did you tell your mother you'd seen Greg stealing silver and cut glass? So as to get rid of him?'

Finally, Zane spoke. 'The man hung around, listening, pretending to be busy, poking his nose in where it wasn't wanted.' He closed his eyes and very gently shook his head. 'You have no idea how difficult it was looking after my mother for all that time when she was ill. Nothing was ever good enough for her. I was trying to set up my business, and all she did was complain.'

'I knew it,' said Sarge from the sofa, loud enough for everyone to hear.

'Over time, I became increasingly angry.' His eye muscle twitched. 'I gave two years of my life to her. Put my relationship on hold. My business took off, but the costs exploded, so I needed more and more money to keep investing in it. Always launching new services and products.' He flashed an angry look at Felix. 'Everything was fine until Becky popped up...'

'Excuse me?' Becky's face was scrunched tight, her eyes narrowed.

'Until Becky came on the scene, there was just me. Mum wanted to make sure she was financially secure while Felix was in prison so I... I took advantage to make sure my family was going to be provided for and secure in the future too.'

'Why did you buy her a yacht?' asked Ellie.

'I didn't.' He snorted. 'It was mine. My accountant advised me to put it in her name.'

'Very strategic. And the will?'

'When Felix came out of prison, he came sniffing round again. Wanting Mum to change her will.'

'Absolutely untrue,' said Felix, his voice simmering with anger. 'I met with your mother *once*, at her request.'

'And you could not tolerate her changing her will to include your father,' Sylvia told Zane, 'or changing the deeds to the farmhouse into his name, because that would scupper your retreat centre plans?'

Zane was silent again.

'So, you went round on Thursday, confronted your mother and killed her?'

He stroked his beard for a few moments, then nodded.

'Was it always your plan to frame me?' Sylvia asked, her tone angry.

'What are you talking about?'

'Did you put up the shrine in the guest room at Mistletoe Manor?'

'No.'

'But you called the police, right? Saying you saw me strangle your mother?'

'He probably used AI,' said Zoe. 'It's really easy to do. You can make a voice sound like whoever you want.'

Dave stepped forward and addressed Zane. 'We'll continue to analyse that recording. We'll also look at the camera Ellie mentioned, don't you worry.'

Zane looked sheepish.

'We will also speak to your mother's solicitor. Zane Wyndham, I am arresting you on suspicion of the murder of Penelope Wyndham. You do not have to say anything, but anything you do say will be taken down and may be given in evidence.'

Zane muttered.

'I shall be instructing our digital officers to run your voice through our AI detection systems. If you made a false police report about my mother, we'll be adding "perverting the course of justice" to your charges.'

Chapter 37 DAY 5 MONDAY

After Zane Wyndham's arrest, Greg went home with Sarge, where he was going to stay until his job was reinstated at Mistletoe Manor. The Blix family stayed up late, discussing the case, and agreed on a slow start in the morning.

It was the 23rd of December and the day of the Christmas fair at Wootton Castle.

Ellie was cooking breakfast for her B&B guests, who were checking out today. Her phone rang. It was Zoe.

'Hey, Mum. What time is the dancing display?'

Ellie switched the loudspeaker on. 'Hold on. The leaflet's here somewhere.' She turned the bacon down and rummaged about on the worktop. 'Here we are. Display by local ice champions, Lara Mullins and Trevor Galloway, 2pm. The sledge rides start at 1pm.' She returned to the hob and the frying pan.

'Shall we get there at 1.30pm then? It's my day off but I've said I'll help with a badger that's got stuck. Finn's going to give me a hand.'

'That works for me. Shall we walk down from here with your gran and Leonard?'

'Yup. Finn wants to go on foot so he can have a few hot spiced ciders. Did you see they've got an icehouse this year with frozen cocktails?'

Ellie chuckled. 'Your gran told me. It does sound rather good.'

'What's Dad doing?'

'He said he'll definitely be there for the ice skating. Got a Morris Dancing rehearsal before that. They're booked for Boxing Day, outside the library.'

Zoe laughed. They'd all wondered how long Dave's Morris Dancing was going to last, but he'd become an enthusiast. Even been on a weekend away, competing in Wales.

'And Sarge and Greg?' asked Zoe.

'They're collecting your great-gran from Sholden.'

Ellie felt a rush of love for her daughter. She always wanted to gather everyone together. It had been a horrible few days. The whole village was looking forward to something fun before Christmas.

After breakfast, Ellie's guests checked out. They declared that, despite all the events of the past few days, they'd enjoyed their stay and would be back. Ellie waved them off, rather nervously wondering if their Trip Advisor review would back this up.

Once their backs disappeared from sight at the bottom of the drive, she pulled her coat on for a leg stretch with Rebus. A fresh dusting of snow covered Pennypot Lane. From someone's open window, the bells of a carol rang out softly. Ellie crossed the lane and stepped onto the green. She let Rebus off his lead and watched him dive forward and roll, enjoying the feel of the cold snow on his body, face and ears – as he'd done ever since he was a puppy.

Four children were building a snowman with what looked like one of their dads. The man was issuing instructions while the children ignored him and excitedly did their own thing.

Over by the pond, on the wooden bench overlooking the water, sat a woman Ellie recognised. Sally. She was throwing the ball for Luna. Luna brought it back and Sally threw it again; not what Sally usually did on a dog walk.

Rebus recognised Luna and charged over, Ellie following. She hadn't properly caught up with her friend since the evening they'd gone round to talk about the Wyndhams and Becky. She'd seen Sally, of course, at Mistletoe Manor the night before, but once Dave arrested Zane, it was already 10.30pm and everyone had gone their separate ways.

'Hi Sal. Are you grabbing a few moments of peace?'

Sally gave her friend a warm smile. 'Morning. Something like that.' She budged up, allowing Ellie room to sit down.

The two dogs were chasing each other, spinning and rolling in the snow, squealing in delight.

'How's your mum?'

Sally nodded. 'Thanks. Not bad. It's been a bit of a shock for all of us, finding out about Becky. We're going to get together with her after Christmas. Meet her family in due course and introduce ours.'

'That sounds promising.'

'She seems nice.'

'Yes.' The second time Ellie had met Becky, her impression had been very different.

'Mum never said anything about getting pregnant and having the baby adopted so, in some ways, it's been more of a shock for me than for her, but we all understand the reasons why she did what she did.'

Ellie heard the pain in her friend's voice. 'I'm really sorry all this had to come out as part of the investigation.' She faced Sally; saw the worry in her intelligent, brown eyes. 'Sylvia and I have always said the worst part of these cases is having to ask our friends and family about things that are either private or uncomfortable.'

'I can imagine.'

'But this is the first time something like this has happened. The first time we've actually pulled friends' skeletons out of the closet.'

'It wasn't anyone's fault, Ells. This was a secret that Mum and Felix had been keeping for many years. When you do that, you run the risk it'll get out. I'd completely forgotten Mum was friends with the Wyndhams.'

'Village life,' said Ellie.

Sally gave a weak smile.

'What are you all up to for Christmas?'

'Pete and I are going round to my parents' on Christmas Day and his on Boxing Day. I gather you're doing Christmas at the windmill again. Pete had a pint with Dave during the week. He was telling Pete how busy you are and that you have to keep cancelling dates.'

Ellie tittered. She'd come to accept there were two types of gossip in villages: that of relative strangers... and the discussion of one's private life that went on between friends, family and people one had grown up with.

'Not intentionally. Or, rather, not with *bad* intentions. Simply that something always seems to come up. Either with the B&B guests, or with the family, or with Blix Blitz... or with the windmill. And Zoe seems to think the house is now a wildlife sanctuary.'

'Aww.'

Ellie told Sally about the deer in the outhouse.

'It's because she feels safe at your place. Everyone does. It's why Sarge has practically moved in and why Greg came back to yours.'

Ellie gave her a play-slap. 'That's such a lovely thing to say. I knew you were my best friend for a reason.'

'Going back to Dave; he's a smart chap,' said Sally. 'I'm sure he understands. He's probably just a bit over-sensitive. You know what he's like. He's so desperate for you guys to get back together, it sounds like he's overthinking. Taking things personally.'

'I'm going to have a chat with him later at the castle. I suspect part of the problem is that he might see three years as a long time, because things are more straightforward for him, but I'm still feeling my way through everything.'

Sally nodded. 'Understandable.'

'Thank you.' She gave her friend an appreciative smile. 'Anyway – will we see you later at the castle?'

'Yes. Pete and I will be there in time for the ice skating. I can't wait. Been a fan of Lara Mullins and Trevor Galloway for about ten years.'

Four hours later, Ellie, Zoe, Sylvia and Leonard sauntered towards the fifteenth- century castle in the village. Zoe had her arm linked through her mum's and Finn had his arm linked through Zoe's. Sylvia and Leonard were holding hands.

In the distance, the stone walls were illuminated by pink and purple lights.

'Wow, so pretty,' said Zoe.

When they got to the castle grounds, the path took them through illuminated stars which were taller than Finn. To the left, a giant snowman was bathed in green and yellow light.

'Does anyone want a sledge ride?' asked Leonard, schoolboy excitement creeping into his voice.

Sylvia squealed. '*Me.* Shall we do one now, before the ice skating starts?'

'Good idea.'

They trundled off, chatting and giggling.

'I'm pleased she's moving on,' announced Finn. 'He's good for her.'

'Me too,' Zoe replied, her eyes wide with excitement. 'What shall we do first? I'm not sure I'm interested in festive stories read by Father Christmas. *Or* Santa's grotto.'

'My stomach's been rumbling for hours,' Finn replied. 'How about finding the alpine bar? They're doing wood-fired pizzas, hot dogs, and churros. And hot, spiced cider.'

'I thought I could smell fruit,' said Ellie.

'And festive cocktails,' Zoe added.

Ellie smiled. Finn and Zoe were always hungry, and it reminded her to eat too, something she forgot sometimes when she was busy. They were just about to head off when, in the shimmering light, and out of sight momentarily, beautiful voices sang, *'Silent Night, Holy Night. All is calm, all is bright...'*

A procession of choristers flowed through a stone arch towards them, bearing fire torches and lanterns, wearing all-white cassocks and surplices.

Ellie gasped and they all sang along.

'Round yon Virgin, Mother and Child...'

Zoe took out her phone and snapped a couple of pictures, and a selfie with Finn.

'Holy Infant so tender and mild...'

They stood to one side, letting the procession pass. Kathy's daughter waved as they went, then one of the ladies from the post office.

'Unless you want to come for some food,' Zoe told Ellie, 'we'll meet you at the lake in fifteen minutes for the ice skating. On the corner by the greenhouse and the kitchen garden, where the giant Christmas tree is.'

Dave was walking towards them, a soft smile on his face.

Ellie's heart somersaulted. He was wearing his grey peacoat and red scarf, face unshaven. He looked tired.

Zoe gave her dad a hug, and she and Finn left them.

'No emergencies, B&B guests and murders this evening then?' Dave teased.

Ellie chuckled. 'Hopefully not. I'm exhausted.' She was aware of a growing desire to feel Dave's arms round her.

'Our daughter assures me the ice bar is rather cool. Can I buy you a drink? Apparently, the warm plum vodka is delicious.'

'How on earth have they built an ice bar?' Ellie's shoulders dropped and she felt herself relaxing, relieved the case was over.

'Let's go and find out. It's in the walled garden.' Dave offered his arm. 'This way, madam.'

They shuffled along the broad walk into the dry moat, and through the arch, stopping to admire the view. The winter light shone through the thin, translucent leaves of the trees. Branches were lit up in an array of colours. Coloured lights bounced off the castle walls. Green, pink and purple water spouted from the fountain. The lily pond was alive with red and blue lights, making the fish look huge. Topiary hedges surrounded the terrace.

'Nothing like cannons to make you feel Christmassy,' Ellie joked, gesturing to the imposing artillery on the castle ramparts at the edge of the terrace.

The icehouse was in a large wooden cabin with two sets of doors to keep the cold in.

Ellie and Dave stepped in and were shown to a booth where a waitress took their order. They sat opposite each other on the ice seats, their drinks on the ice table, chatting about the family and Christmas.

When their drinks arrived, Ellie took a sip of her plum vodka. 'Mmm.'

Dave had a cheeky twinkle in his eye. 'We've spoken to the Selbys. They found the items Penelope accused Greg of stealing, in the garage. They've reinstated Greg, although he's decided to live out from now on – at Sarge's.'

'Ah. I'm very pleased to hear that. Now Sean's moved out, and is having his own family, the two men will be great company for each other.'

'We've interviewed Toby. He's admitted he went to Mistletoe Manor to tell Penelope he was re-starting legal proceedings against her. We are reopening the investigation into who jumped him in the alley. We strongly suspect this was Zane but need evidence to charge him. We also have a match on the voice that rang saying they'd seen Mum strangling Penelope.'

'Zane?'

'Yup. He's going to prison for a very long time.'

'Good,' said Ellie.

'And Felix?'

'It's going to take a while to look into all the new evidence he's given us, but it looks like he was telling the truth about Penelope putting him up to the art fraud. At least he can get on with his life now and Beech Farm will be his.'

'That's a good outcome too.'

'We've been analysing Penelope's emails and a journal she kept. She'd been digging up information on Mum, and been quietly sewing seeds of doubt about her amongst Mum's acquaintances.'

Ellie groaned. 'That's awful.'

'We'll probably never fully know what she was up to where Mum was concerned, but it's clear she wanted to cause trouble for her and sully her reputation.'

'Why though? Penelope wasn't affected financially by Felix's conviction.'

'She wasn't, but she felt her standing in the community had been affected badly. We found journal entries where she talked about people shunning her and gossiping about her.'

'What's that got to do with Sylvia?'

'Jealousy, pure and simple. We only examined one journal, but she mentions Mum *twenty-seven* times. Saying how it's "alright for her" because she's a cop's wife and can't do any wrong. How everyone loves Mum, referring to her as "Mrs Perfect", making snide comments about her grandchildren.'

'What an odd business,' said Ellie. 'Jealousy is so destructive.'

It was always distressing when a member of their community died. Penelope hadn't been popular, but her death had still sent shockwaves through the village.

'I feel sorry for Zane's wife and children,' said Ellie.

'Yes. They're going to move away, I gather. Start afresh somewhere where the children won't be hounded for what their father has done.'

'I'm pleased. Changing the subject – will you come for Christmas lunch on Wednesday? It's going to be a full house, as usual.'

A grin spread over Dave's face. 'I'd love that. Thanks.'

'I'm sorry I've had to cancel so many of our arrangements recently.' Ellie wanted to be honest with Dave as well as with herself. She waited to see how *he* would respond and how *she* would feel.

'It's OK.' He cupped his bristly cheeks in his hands. 'I have felt a bit disappointed because I was looking forward to seeing you. But each time it's happened, it's been obvious that something genuine had come up, so it wasn't as if I felt you were messing me about or trying to get out of plans.'

Ellie caught Dave's gaze and lingered there for a few moments, basking in the warmth and affection she knew so well. It was tempting to fall into his arms and agree to a reconciliation, but she wasn't ready for that yet.

'It *definitely* wasn't either of those. I enjoy the time we spend together.' She met his gaze again. 'I always have.'

'But?'

'I don't know if there is a but...'

'It feels like it's "I enjoy the time we spend together *but...*"'

Ellie frowned, trying to figure out how she felt. 'I think it's just that I'm so busy. My days are one thing after another. That probably sounds corny, and I know your schedule is pressured too, but I'm still getting used to having the B&B guests, and I'm figuring out ways of handling all the various situations that come up; learning how to prioritise and set boundaries.'

This was the first time she'd analysed her feelings in this amount of detail. Up until now, she'd been simply getting on with it all. 'So, it's more like an "and". I enjoy the time we spend together *and* I'm enjoying new projects, new horizons.'

She told him about the fuse board and the mouse.

'I know I shouldn't laugh,' said Dave, stifling a chuckle. 'I'd love to have seen that mouse though and your guest's face.'

'I had to be there to sort that out. Zoe is flat-out with her new job. Sylvia is busy with Leonard. It's down to me to make sure the B&B guests are happy and safe, and have everything they need.'

Dave nodded.

'I guess that's one of the occupational hazards of being a B&B host,' Ellie continued. 'I might've just ordered a pizza and a glass of wine somewhere, and my phone will ring saying a guest has locked themselves out. Or a cleaning client has an issue. I'll always have to drop what I'm doing.'

'You'll get your systems in place. I'm sure of it. And people to help you.' Dave shifted in his seat. 'I suppose…' He cleared his throat. 'I suppose what I'm wondering is whether you're using those crises as a way to stop our relationship from moving forward?'

Ellie's stomach lurched. Was this what she'd felt uneasy about?

'I'm putting you on the spot,' Dave added, 'so you don't have to answer that now. Have a think about it.'

'I will. I probably *am* happier about things moving more slowly than you.'

'That's what worries me.'

Ellie paused. The conversation was making her tense. 'It shouldn't. If you think about it, it makes sense. We've agreed all along that moving on from your affair – and potentially getting back together – is more straightforward for you. For me… it's complex and it's only been three years.'

Dave's face tightened.

'It still feels like your fling with Andrea was only yesterday.' As she spoke, she realised that was it: her feelings were still a bit raw.

'But we hardly see each other. It seems to be snatched moments here and there.'

Ellie saw the pain in Dave's face.

'If it makes you feel better, that's pretty much how it is with Sylvia and Zoe. Half an hour here and there. A meal together. Collapsing in front of the telly.'

He released a sigh.

'It wouldn't be any different if we were living together. I'd still have to sort things out with cleaning customers and B&B guests.' Ellie paused and reached for his hand. 'What part of this bothers you? Can you tell me?'

Dave pursed his lips as though he was deciding whether to say more. 'I think I'm scared that I want to get back together more than you. And maybe, taking that a step further, I'm worried that it's not what you want after all.'

Panic gripped Ellie. Was that true?

Dave must've seen her face. 'Oh, my goodness. That's it, isn't it? You don't want to.'

'I… er… No, *no*, it's not that.' She gathered her thoughts. 'This conversation has whooshed off in a weird direction. I don't want to say something I don't feel.'

He stared at her, searching her face for answers.

'It's not that I *don't* want to get back together.' She was trying to connect with her feelings and decide how to articulate them. 'It's that I don't *know* what I want yet. I'm happy that we're going on dates and that we're not just mates now, but I don't want more than that at the moment.'

Dave was soaking up every word.

'I'm not ready. And I can't say what I'm going to want in the future because I don't know, and I don't want to give you false hope.' She met his eyes again so he would see she was telling the truth. 'But – that's very different from not wanting it. It's a process I've got to go through.'

Dave gulped.

'However, while I might not know what the future will look like, but I do know it involves y–'

The door opened.

'Come on, you two. The–' Zoe broke off.

Dave closed his eyes and groaned.

'What's going on?' She stared first at Ellie then Dave.

'Nothing,' Ellie replied hastily. 'We were just talking.'

Zoe frowned. 'The ice skating is about to start.'

Ellie and Dave drained their drinks and followed Zoe out of the cabin and made it to the pond just as two figures took to the ice.

Sarge had arrived with Sylvia's mother, Mary, and Greg.

'Gran,' Dave said to Mary. 'How are you?'

'Between us, we've just eaten half a hazelnut praline Yule log,' she said with a twinkle in her eye, 'a cranberry and cinnamon scone each and had a delicious glass of fizz.'

Dave sniggered. 'That good, huh?'

Sarge brought out the best in Sylvia's mother. He always had.

'"Come along to a winter wonderland of lights and pyrotechnics," these two told me,' said Mary. 'I've brought my trusty picnic seat.'

Right on cue, Greg held up a foldable metal and canvas seat.

The lights focussed on the two skaters.

The two figures took up their positions, backs together, one skate tilted.

Zoe squealed. 'Here we go.'

On the other side of the pond, Ellie saw Becky and her family, and Felix with his new partner. She waved at them and settled in to enjoy the show.

When the performance finished, the family wandered round the walled garden, enjoying the pink and purple glow on the trees and the exposed brickwork.

The lights were on in the greenhouse and Ellie went in. There were rows of plants on benches in various phases of growth and potting. Several watering cans and bags of feed and plastic pots. She spotted Sarge, chatting to a young man in overalls.

'The trick with these is to use a grow lamp,' Sarge told the lad, who was listening eagerly. 'Stops the seedlings from getting leggy, it does. Doesn't force them but gives them that little boost. Helps them grow strong.' He saw Ellie and smiled. 'He's doing an apprenticeship. I'm going to be volunteering here in the new year, and he'll be one of my charges.'

The apprentice felt in the pot with his fingers and added another handful of compost.

'With things like aubergines and chillies,' Sarge continued, 'a heated propagator works a treat.'

Ellie left them to it, ambling along the rows. The conversation with Dave had left her feeling unsettled, particularly since she hadn't been able to finish her sentence. Sally's mother's words floated into her mind: 'Don't let him slip through your fingers, will you?' The constant questions from friends and family, while understandable and well-meant, made her worry that a clock was ticking; that Dave was going to get fed up with her and find someone else. She needed to tell him that, although she wasn't sure what shape her future was going to take, she was *certain* it involved him.

She took in the tables of plants and seeds, all doing their own thing, growing at their own pace, responding to a sprinkle of feed here and a blast of heat there. She chuckled as she remembered the multi-socket adapter, which her B&B guests had brought. Zoe bringing a deer home. The cleaning rota she was managing every day. It was a good life. Four months ago, she'd wanted new challenges and new horizons, and she'd got them. She was still finding her way with her guests, but she had choices and that was what she'd wanted. If being a host wasn't for her, she could stop. And if she didn't experiment, she wouldn't know.

Zoe was stepping out into the world and creating new experiences for herself every day. Sylvia had been shaken by Penelope's death. It had brought up the past – but she was back on track and slowly moving on. She had gone through a period of not knowing what she wanted too. She'd tried new things, grieved, waited, got angry, shed tears... and finally been ready to move forward. It wasn't that Ellie didn't want to get back together with Dave. It was that she wasn't ready to be in a live-in relationship with *anyone* at the moment.

Through the glass of the greenhouse, Ellie caught sight of Zoe and Finn, cheeks flushed, squealing with joy, throwing snowballs at each other. With her new job and home, Zoe was navigating changes too. So was Finn, who'd shared his house with a buddy for two years and now had Zoe living there.

Ellie glanced over at Sarge, who was still helping the castle's apprentice. Sarge was responding to developments, with his nephew moving out. His old friend, Greg, had left the manor house, where he'd lived for decades and was moving in – adjustments for him too.

Perhaps that was what life was about...? Everyone responding to change in their own time and way. In which case – wasn't that what Ellie was doing too?

The End.

If you enjoyed Ellie, Zoe and Sylvia's story in this book, you can follow their adventures in the next one, *Murder at Badger Brook*, which is available on Amazon here.

This is the blurb...

MURDER AT BADGER BROOK

Will curiosity be Ellie's downfall?

Winter is receding in Lower Wootton. Ellie Blix is relieved her daughter's job is settling down, so it's a shock for everyone when Zoe finds a dead body amongst the snowdrops at Badger Brook, while she's rescuing an animal.

The victim has no ID on him. The village rumour mill soon declares he's the homeless man that's been stealing from the corner shop, and lurking around people's barns.

Ellie quickly discovers the dead man was a once-wealthy aristocrat, Marcus Davenport, who went missing after a mysterious car crash ten years ago. But if he was alive until recently, how could his death have been registered a few years after his disappearance?

With no shortage of suspects, Ellie must sift through petty rivalries and village gossip to get to the truth… and find out how a man who was supposed to be dead, has just been killed.

Order *Murder at Badger Brook* here.

A note from the author

Dear reader,

Thank you so much for reading this book. It has been a lot of fun to write. Without you, however, it would simply be words in a document on my hard drive.

It is immensely gratifying that so many of you have taken the characters and stories from *The Wootton Windmill Mysteries* into your homes and hearts. Many of you have taken the time to email and tell me what the stories have meant to you. I read and reply to each one.

Getting news first

The best way to keep in touch is to join my newsletter. This is where I share news first, including exclusive offers, early reads, 'behind the scenes' & giveaways. You can join here.

Supporting the series

You can do this in three ways:

a) If you've enjoyed this story, please tell your friends, family, book clubs, and online groups about the series. It's easy to underestimate what this can do, but word of mouth is one of the best forms of marketing.

b) Another way to help is by leaving a quick, written review on Amazon. Amazon prompts us to leave a rating when we finish a book on kindle, and the average rating is important. However, a few lines saying what you liked about the story helps other readers to know what the book is like.

c) By pre-ordering the next in the series, which you can do here.

Please note: I am a British writer and I write using British English. This story is set in an English village and the manuscript has been edited and proofread by British professionals. A few spellings, terms and words may, therefore, be different for some readers. I've tried to ensure, however, that the meaning is clear for everyone. In addition, the stories are intended to be lighthearted reads. They aren't police procedurals and the sleuths do things detectives aren't allowed to do. This is intentional and is meant to be part of the fun of a cosy mystery.

I get a lot of emails and messages asking me if Lower Wootton is a real place. It isn't. Sorry. It is a fictional village which I've created by borrowing elements of many villages, mixing them up and fictionalising them. If you try to plot places, you will find I've moved them, changed them and given them different names!

Finally, writing a novel is a team effort. I come up with the plot and characters, and write the words, and other people contribute at various stages. Without their input and magic, this story would not have made it into print.

I owe massive thanks to the following people for their help. In no particular order: Scott Pack, Louise Voss, Ken Dawson, Matthew J Evans, Lynne Nazareth, Lucy Lawrie, Neil Baker, Louise Mangos. Thanks also to Liz and Keith Atkinson who own Ripple Windmill, the inspiration for Ellie, Sylvia and Zoe's home in the series. Thanks, too, to Ian Rankin, whose crime novels I've devoured for years.

The name of Ellie's dog is a tribute to Ian's detective.

Finally, to all my early and beta readers – thank you.

Sincere apologies to anyone I've forgotten.

About the author

Izzie Harper is the pen name of British writer, teacher & story coach, Vicky Newham. Vicky lives on the south coast of England.

As Izzie Harper, she writes *The Wootton Windmill Mysteries.*

Vicky's first crime fiction series was published by HQ/Harper Collins. Her debut in this police procedural series, *Turn a Blind Eye*, was optioned for TV and was shortlisted for the CWA John Creasey Debut Dagger in 2019. She has MAs in Creative Writing and Effective Learning.

To keep up to date with Vicky's releases, special offers and promotions, please join her newsletter here.

If you like pictures of dogs, the sea, the Kent countryside and behind-the-scenes of Vicky's writing, you can follow her on Twitter at @VickyNewham and on Instagram at @vickynewhamwriter.

If you have enjoyed this story, Vicky would be hugely grateful if you could leave a quick review on Amazon and if you could tell your family and friends about it. Reviews and word-of-mouth recommendations are the best way to help authors.

And, please pre-order book 8, *Murder at Badger Brook*, here.

Printed in Great Britain
by Amazon

52454785R00189